Welcome to The Grand View, Hannah!

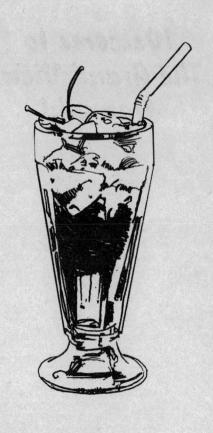

Welcome to The Grand View, Hannah!

by
Mindy Warshaw Skolsky

Illustrated by Patrick Faricy

Previously published as *Hannah Is a Palindrome*

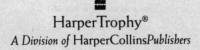

HarperTrophy®
A Division of HarperCollinsPublishers

Harper Trophy® is a registered trademark of HarperCollins Publishers Inc.

Welcome to The Grand View, Hannah!
Text copyright © 2000 by Mindy Warshaw Skolsky
Illustrations copyright © 2000 by Patrick Faricy

Library of Congress Cataloging-in-Publication Data
Skolsky, Mindy Warshaw.
 [Hannah is a palindrome]
 Welcome to the Grand View, Hannah! / by Mindy Warshaw Skolsky ; illustrated by Patrick Faricy.
    p.   cm.
 Summary: Living in rural New York state during the 1930's, Hannah begins to see her parents and herself in a different light as they settle into their new apartment behind the Grand View Restaurant.
 ISBN 0-06-440785-3 (pbk.)
 [1. Family life—New York (State)—Fiction.   2. Restaurants—Fiction.   3. Country life—New York (State)—Fiction.   4. New York (State)—Fiction.]   I. Faricy, Patrick, ill.
II. Title.
PZ7.S62836We   2000   99-23891
[Fic]—dc21   CIP
                                                                                  AC

First Harper Trophy edition, 2000

Previously published as *Hannah Is a Palindrome* 1980

Visit us on the World Wide Web!
www.harperchildrens.com

To the memory
of Mollie and Izzie, again,
because this book is really
about them.

With special thanks to
Morris J. Markowitz and Rose Golod Bonn
for their helpful recollections
of passementerie.

Welcome to
The Grand View,
Hannah!

Surprise!

On a beautiful warm day in Indian summer, Hannah's father told Hannah and her mother he had something he wanted to show them.

"It's a surprise," he said.

"Hooray!" said Hannah. She loved her father's surprises.

Hannah's mother looked worried. She didn't love Hannah's father's surprises as much as Hannah did.

"What is it?" asked Hannah's mother.

"You'll see," said Hannah's father. "If I tell you, it won't be a surprise."

They went out to their little black car and got in. Hannah sat in the middle. They drove up to

7
GALLONS
FOR
$1

the top of their street and turned left on Route 9W. Then they drove from Nyack to Grand View, which was right next to Nyack.

Soon they came to a little restaurant with two blue-and-yellow gasoline pumps. Hannah's father turned left again and parked the car between the gasoline pumps and the restaurant. A big sign said 7 GALLONS FOR $1. Hannah read it out loud.

"Are we going to get gas?" asked Hannah's mother. "Is that the surprise?"

"You'll see," said Hannah's father.

They went into the little restaurant.

Inside, a man was leaning on a large green metal box.

"Hello again!" said the man to Hannah's father. He stood up straight and put his hand out. Hannah's father shook hands with him.

"This is my wife and daughter," said Hannah's father. "Would you show them how that soda box works? They'll have to see it to believe it."

"Soda!" said Hannah. "Is that the surprise?"

Hannah just loved soda. Most of the time her

mother didn't let her have any because Hannah drank it too fast and got a stomachache.

"You'll see," said Hannah's father.

The man reached under a counter next to the soda box and took a bottle of soda from the top of a pile.

"Feel," he said to Hannah. "Warm or cold?"

Hannah felt the soda bottle. "Warm," she said. She looked at the bottle cap. "It's a warm Dr. Pepper."

The man opened a metal flap on the right side of the big green soda box. Under the flap was a row of holes. Then he opened a flap on the left side of the soda box. Under that flap was another row of holes.

The man pushed the bottle of soda into one of the holes on the right side—and a bottle of soda popped up out of a hole on the left side. "Abracadabra!" he said. He reached over and took the bottle out. "Feel," he said to Hannah. "Warm or cold?"

Hannah felt the bottle. "Cold!" she said. "It's ice-cold Dr. Pepper! How did you do that?"

The man opened a door on the top of the box. He turned a wooden crate upside down so Hannah could stand on it. "Look inside," he said. The inside of the soda box was filled with water, and in the middle of the water was the biggest chunk of ice Hannah had ever seen.

"It looks just like a picture of an iceberg Miss Pepper showed us in school!" she said.

"Well, around and under that big chunk of ice," said the man, "is a row of metal tubes. There's a tube for every flavor of soda: one for orange, one for cream, one for lemon-lime, ginger ale, Coca-Cola, root beer, Dr. Pepper, and sarsaparilla."

"Oh, *sarsaparilla!*" said Hannah.

"Already I don't like the sounds of this," said Hannah's mother under her breath. "Your father always falls in love with gadgets, and it always costs us money."

"Ma, shh!" Hannah whispered back. "The man will hear you!"

Hannah loved gadgets too. She held her breath and watched the soda box.

"The tubes go down, under, and up the other

side," the man continued. "When I put a warm bottle in on the right side, it pushes all the other bottles in the tube till one pops up on the left side. Those other bottles have been in there awhile, and they get chilled from that 'iceberg' that's inside the box."

"What an invention!" said Hannah's father. "Even if I didn't make it myself, I have to say I never saw something like it."

Hannah's father made inventions. Hannah and her father always thought his inventions were wonderful.

Hannah let her breath out.

"Are we buying the soda box?" she asked. "Is that the surprise?"

"We're buying the whole place," said Hannah's father. "Surprise!"

"Oh, *hooray*!" said Hannah.

"We're *what*?" said Hannah's mother.

"You know where everything is," said the man to Hannah's father. "I'll let you show your wife around by yourself. You probably want privacy." The man disappeared.

Now Hannah's father looked worried.

"Wait," he said to Hannah's mother. "Wait till you see the rest of it. It's a real bargain. You'll love it."

"I don't love such surprises," said Hannah's mother. "I like to know about things in advance."

"I didn't know we were buying a restaurant," said Hannah.

"We aren't yet," said her mother.

"But we talked about buying a little business," said Hannah's father to Hannah's mother, "where I could be my own boss." Hannah's father didn't like anybody to tell him what to do.

"But I like to be my own boss too," said Hannah's mother. "Things should be fifty-fifty in a marriage. This is 1932. I like to be modern."

"Well, I would never sign anything without you," said Hannah's father. "I didn't sign any papers. The reason I didn't say anything is I wanted to surprise you."

"Okay," said Hannah's mother. "One of these days I'll faint from one of your surprises. So show me."

"Show me too," said Hannah.

"Well, naturally," said her father. "Did you think we would leave you out?"

"Wait till I write to Grandma and Grandpa!" said Hannah. "Will *they* be surprised! That would be *two* moves. They moved from Nyack back to the Bronx. And we might move from Nyack to Grand View."

"Don't write any letters yet," said Hannah's mother. "So far we didn't move."

Hannah looked at her father. He winked at her.

"We *might* . . ." thought Hannah.

Hannah's mother always started out saying no to Hannah's father's surprises.

But Hannah knew that most of the time her mother ended up saying yes.

"So *maybe* . . ." said Hannah to herself. She crossed her fingers. And she winked back at her father.

Fifty-fifty

The restaurant had five tables. Each table had four chairs. Between the restaurant and the soda box there was a candy case. Next to the candy case was the cash register.

"That would be your job," said Hannah's father to Hannah's mother. "Just to sit by the register and count the money. I would do everything else."

Hannah's mother was very good at arithmetic. She always took care of the checkbook because she used to be a bookkeeper. Hannah's father didn't like arithmetic. He never remembered to write his checks in the book. When he forgot, Hannah's mother called him "absentminded professor." Even when he remembered, Hannah's mother still had to fix a lot of numbers in the checkbook.

"Oh, what's a little mistake?" Hannah's father always said. "Everybody makes mistakes."

Hannah's father went over to the front counter next to the soda box.

"This counter is for outside customers," he said. "The ones in a hurry who don't have time to come inside. Or for customers who like to be out in the fresh air."

"Like you!" said Hannah.

Hannah's father liked fresh air so much, Hannah's mother called him a fresh-air fiend.

"Now come and see the kitchen," said Hannah's father.

The kitchen was large and so was everything in it: the big black stove, the worktable, the white refrigerator.

"The walls are really dark from grease in here," said Hannah's mother. "They have to be washed and painted."

"We can do that," said Hannah's father. "I'm a

good painter. Now follow me. Here comes the beauty of it."

They stepped from the kitchen into the living room.

"You don't have to pay rent for rooms," said Hannah's father. "Because you live here too."

There was a large grate in the middle of the floor.

Hannah went over to look at it.

"That's where the heat comes from," said her father.

Hannah's mother went over and looked at it too.

"Instead of radiators," said Hannah's father.

"Oh, look over there in the corner," said Hannah. "A piano!"

Her mother turned around. "A *piano!*" she said. She walked over to the corner.

"That's a *special* kind of piano," said Hannah's father in a loud voice.

The man popped up again.

"That's a player piano," he said. "It has rolls."

"What are piano rolls?" asked Hannah.

"Wait till you see *this*," said her father. "It's as good as the soda box."

The man slid open two little doors over the keyboard. There were round metal rods inside. He opened the piano bench and took out a long roll of white paper. He put it inside the opening and fitted it over the round metal rods. He sat down and began to pump some pedals with his feet. The white paper roll began to unwind. Hannah saw little holes in the paper. Then she heard music.

"I know that!" she said. "That's 'Bye Bye Blackbird.'"

The man pushed a button.

"Look!" said Hannah. "The keys are going up and down."

"You can play it two ways," said the man. "With the keys straight, or going up and down like this if you want to make believe you're playing."

"Oh, can *I*?" asked Hannah.

"Be my guest," said the man.

Hannah sat down and moved her hands up and down the keyboard. "I'm playing the piano!" she said. She pumped and played till she came to the end of the song.

After the last note of the song, the piano keys went up and down and made four extra sounds. It sounded to Hannah like "di da di *dum!*" Then it stopped.

"Does that piano go with the place?" asked Hannah's mother.

"For twenty dollars," said the man.

"Twenty dollars!" said Hannah's mother. "For twenty dollars, you could sell it to Rockefeller!"

"Well, I'll give you privacy to look at the rest of the place now," said the man. He took the roll out of the piano, put it back in the bench, closed the sliding doors over the keyboard, and disappeared again.

As soon as he left, Hannah started to sing the words to "Bye Bye Blackbird."

"Why didn't you sing along with the roll?" asked her mother.

"I was embarrassed in front of the man," said Hannah. She did a shuffle off to Buffalo. "If we lived here, I could play 'Bye Bye Blackbird' on the piano and sing and get up and tap-dance after I finished."

"If we lived here," said her mother, "you could take piano lessons and learn the 'Blue Danube' waltz. But he should throw the piano in with the place."

"Shh, Ma," said Hannah. "He'll hear you."

"So what's wrong?" asked her mother. "It's the truth."

"Look at these French doors," said Hannah's father, walking over to the end of the living room. "Aren't they a pair of beauties?"

Hannah walked over to her father.

"Glass doors with little crisscross panes," she said. "I like that kind."

"They're a nuisance to wash," said Hannah's mother. "Where do they go to?"

"Outside," said Hannah's father. "But he keeps them locked."

"Why?" asked Hannah's mother.

"Well, the place is built on the side of a hill and the hill is steep. If you opened the French doors and stepped out, you'd fall out and down."

"So the French doors go no place. What's the idea of doors that go no place?"

"When the place was built, he planned to have a porch added on later. But he never got around to it."

"I think glass doors that go no place are *mysterious!*" said Hannah.

"Come, I'll show you the rest of the place," said her father.

They went behind the living room to see the bedrooms.

"Look in this one," said Hannah. "It has such a big desk! That's the biggest desk I ever saw!"

"That's a rolltop," said Hannah's father. He showed her how the top rolled up and down. Under the top, there were a lot of little cubbyholes.

"Look at all those cubbies!" said Hannah. "I could keep all my secret things in there. I could draw and paint and write letters to Grandma. That's the best desk I ever saw!"

"There's another one just like it in the garage next to the gas pumps," said her father. "I could

make myself a little office in there. It would be a wonderful place to write letters to the editor." Hannah's father read lots of newspapers and magazines and always wrote letters about things he didn't agree with.

"The wallpaper's old and peeling in here," said Hannah's mother, "but the room is nice and sunny."

"That's because it's on the east side," said Hannah's father.

"Then this would be a good bedroom for Hannah," said her mother. "If it had new wallpaper."

Hannah looked at her father. He winked at her again.

Hannah's mother saw him. "I just meant *if* . . ." she said. "We have to be very careful. It took such a long time to save up."

Hannah's mother liked to think things over calmly and carefully.

Hannah's father liked to do things right at the moment he thought of doing them.

They looked at the other bedroom.

"This one has terrible wallpaper too," said Hannah's mother. "It's half falling off."

"Wallpaper can be changed," said Hannah's father.

They looked at the bathroom in between the two bedrooms.

"There are no radiators in the bedrooms or in the bathroom," said Hannah's mother.

"Who needs radiators?" asked Hannah's father. "Cold air is healthy. Besides, the heat coming up through the grate in the living room warms the whole place."

They went outside to look at the gas station. There was an overhead shed that went from the pumps to the garage. Inside the garage, in one corner, was the other big desk. "This corner would be my office," said Hannah's father. "Where I'd write my letters." Outside on one side of the garage was a small building with two doors. One door said MEN and one door said LADIES.

"You would just sit at the cash register in the restaurant," Hannah's father told Hannah's mother again. "I would pump the gas and do the cooking."

"And write letters to the editor," said Hannah's

mother. "A person can't do three things at once."

"I'd run back and forth," said Hannah's father.

Hannah's father liked to cook. He liked to do a lot of other things too. He liked to do carpentry and make things out of wood. He liked to paint things with enamel paint. He liked to make inventions and call them "my patents."

"This place needs a lot of work," said Hannah's mother. "Inside and out. Look how the fence is falling down. Between the restaurant and the garage."

"But it's such a bargain," said Hannah's father.

"That's probably why," said Hannah's mother. "It would be a better bargain if he would throw in the piano. The place itself is not so hot."

"But I can fix things," said Hannah's father. "You know I'm good at fixing things. I could build a new fence. It would go from the restaurant to the gas station. And I would paint it white. And make some signs. And I'd make a garden by the gas station for my zinnias. We could have two gardens. You could have a separate one just for all your flowers you always wanted."

Hannah's mother loved all different kinds of flowers. Hannah's father loved just one kind: zinnias.

"A garden . . ." said Hannah's mother. She was quiet a minute. Then she said, "But where would I put it? I don't see anyplace with enough room."

"Come and look at the other side of the place," said Hannah's father. They walked back to the restaurant. On the other side there was another falling-down fence and a gate.

"I'd fix this fence too," said Hannah's father quickly. "And make a new gate."

"Where does the gate go to?" asked Hannah.

Her father opened it. Hannah looked down and saw a cement stairway going downhill. She looked up at the side of the building. "There are the French doors!" she said, pointing.

"No wonder he keeps them locked," said her mother. "If you stepped out of the living room through those doors, you'd fall five feet down the cement steps and break your neck! Where do these stairs lead down to, anyway?"

"They go to the cellar," said Hannah's father.

"What cellar?" asked Hannah's mother. "I didn't see any door to the cellar when we were looking at the rooms."

"There aren't any inside stairs," said Hannah's father. "A little mistake when the place was built. But you know me. I could invent an inside stairway."

"That would be some invention," said Hannah's mother. "How would you do that?"

"Oh," said Hannah's father. "I'd think of something. Maybe I could cut an opening in the floor in one of the rooms."

"But we'd fall through the opening into the cellar."

"I'd invent something so we wouldn't."

They started to walk down the outside steps.

Hannah's mother looked over at the side of the hill.

"Here's where I'd plant my garden," she said. "Right here on the hillside. All around that little tree."

"Ooh, that tree is ugly," said Hannah.

"It's still a tree," said her mother. "A garden is a very special thing. Flowers can make you forget ugliness."

Hannah and her father stared at Hannah's mother.

"I mean *if* we take the place," she said. "It doesn't mean we will."

When they got to the bottom of the stairway, Hannah saw railroad tracks just below the building.

"That could be noisy," said her mother. "The train just below the bedrooms."

"How long does the Erie Railroad take to pass by?" asked Hannah's father. "Just a minute."

"A minute each time it passes by," said Hannah's mother. "I hope the whole place doesn't slide down the hill and land on the tracks when the train goes by."

"Then we could sell sodas to the passengers," said Hannah's father.

"You always make jokes!" said Hannah.

Her father opened the door to the cellar. "Here's where I'd put my workbench and tools," he said. "Here's where I'd make my signs and inventions."

"I thought you said you'd be the cook and pump the gas," said Hannah's mother. "And I would just sit at the cash register."

"But when there are no customers," said Hannah's father, "we could work on our gardens and I could make inventions. When customers come in, you could call me."

"I would call you," said Hannah. "And I would work the soda box. And I'd like a garden too. I'd plant green peppers."

"You would go to school," said Hannah's mother.

"Oh, I forgot," said Hannah. "But I mean after school. And on weekends and holidays."

Hannah's mother and father talked awhile. Hannah's mother wanted to think it over. Hannah's father wanted to buy it right away.

"It's a big step," said Hannah's mother. "We saved for such a long time."

"But it's a bargain," said Hannah's father.

They went back up the outside steps and inside the restaurant again.

Hannah's mother kept looking around. She walked in and out of the rooms.

"It isn't very cheerful-looking," she said. "The wood is all so dark. The wallpaper's gray and peeling. I like a place that looks cheerful."

"We could make it cheerful," said Hannah's father. "I could paint dark things light. Branagan can paper. And we could buy one or two cheerful things. From Brown's Furniture. From the money we would save not having to pay rent."

"Branagan is a terrible paperhanger," said Hannah's mother. "But he *is* cheap. And it would be clean and new."

"I love Mr. Branagan," said Hannah. "Say yes! I like it here. I'd like to live behind a little restaurant with a soda box and play the player piano and tap-dance and draw pictures at that big roll-top desk in the bedroom. And grow green peppers!"

"And don't forget the beauty of it," said

Hannah's father. "There's no rent for rooms. The rooms go with the place."

"It would be more beautiful if he would throw in the piano free," said Hannah's mother.

Suddenly the man popped up again.

"Maybe I would throw in the piano with the place," he said. "No extra charge. The desks too."

"It would be the first place we have that's our own," said Hannah's father. Hannah's mother looked at him. Then she looked at the man. She looked at Hannah.

"And I could have my garden," she said quietly. But she wasn't saying it to Hannah's father. She wasn't saying it to the man. She wasn't even saying it to Hannah. "A piano for Hannah and a garden for me," she said. And suddenly Hannah's mother said, "All right."

"Hooray!" yelled Hannah. "It's fifty-fifty!"

The man went over to the soda box. He asked Hannah her favorite flavor. "A celebration," he said.

"Sarsaparilla," said Hannah. She looked at her

mother. She knew she wasn't allowed to have soda between meals.

"You can have half a sarsaparilla," said her mother, "for a special occasion. The rest you can save for after supper. But drink slowly so you don't get a bellyache."

"Ma," whispered Hannah. "Don't say 'bellyache' in front of the man!"

"Come into the living room," said the man. "I'll put my other roll on the piano."

Hannah started her soda. She drank through two straws.

"Oh, I know that too," she said, as the man pumped and the music began to come out. "That's 'Alexander's Ragtime Band.'" The man got up and let Hannah pump the rest of it. After the last note of the song, the piano keys went "di da di *dum!*" again and the man put the roll away. Then he put the bottlecap back on Hannah's soda and gave her two new straws in a wrapper, and Hannah's father gave the man twenty-five dollars for a deposit.

"Until we sign the papers," he said.

"Twenty-five dollars," said Hannah to herself. "I never saw so much money in my whole life."

"I hope we're doing the right thing," said Hannah's mother.

"Don't worry," said Hannah's father. "You worry too much. Why don't you be like me? I never worry."

"That's why I worry so much," said Hannah's mother. "I worry for both of us."

"You'll just sit by the cash register and count the money," said Hannah's father.

When they went outside to their little black car, Hannah got in the middle again. She put the wrapper with the new straws in her lap and held on tightly to the sarsaparilla bottle.

"I like to sit in the middle between my mother and father," she thought as they drove back down Route 9W. "It's cozy."

Hannah's father drove slowly as they went from Grand View back to Nyack on the beautiful warm day in Indian summer, and Hannah knew it was a very special day.

"We just bought a little restaurant," she said to

herself. "With a player piano and a rolltop desk and a soda box. And now we're going to live there."

And she started a letter to her grandmother in her head before she even got to a pad and pencil.

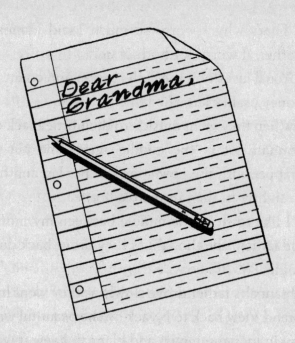

A Letter to Grandma

Dear Grandma,

I'm sorry you moved back to the Bronx. I know it was hard for Grandpa to go back and forth by bus every day and it was too much work taking care of the candy store all by himself. But I miss you both very much. I have no one to play school with now. So I'm sending you homework and we can play school in the mail.

Guess what!

You'll never guess what, so I'll tell you.

We're moving too! We just bought a little restaurant!

When we got back home from buying it, my father said he had another surprise to show us. My mother said, "What now?" The new surprise was a great big piece of wood. It was painted white. It was nice and shiny. It had red trim around the edges. There were a lot of capital letters lying on it. They were all made of wood too. My father made every letter himself. They were painted red and they were shiny too. All except the question marks and periods. My father moved all the letters around on the big white piece of wood until this is what they said:

HUNGRY? THIRSTY?
STOP HERE.

THE GRAND VIEW RESTAURANT.

My mother said that was really counting his chickens before they were hatched. But my father said it wasn't because he didn't nail the letters on until she saw the restaurant and said yes. He's nailing them on right now while I'm writing this. But he's saving the question marks and periods so I can paint them. And when we move to the restaurant, my father's going to nail the whole sign on top of the roof and I'll go to school on the bus and take piano lessons. I'll still go to my same school, but I won't be able to walk with the kids from my old block. I'll be glad to get rid of that pest Otto Zimmer, but I'll miss Aggie Branagan. But I'll still sit next to Aggie in class. I hope I can find my same

place up on top of the mountain where I
like to go sit after school.

 I had half a bottle of sarsaparilla!
                              Love,
                              Hannah
P.S. Do your homework.

Raisins and Almonds

Hannah sat on the school bus and looked out the window at the sign on the roof:

HUNGRY? THIRSTY?
STOP HERE.
THE GRAND VIEW RESTAURANT.

The bus stopped and Hannah got off.

She kept looking up at the sign. "Boy, those question marks and periods really look good," she thought.

She walked over to the restaurant and peeked in through the big glass windows to make sure there were no customers at the tables inside. Then she went over to the counter and looked in through the open window.

"I'm hungry! I'm thirsty!" she yelled. "So I stopped here. At *The Grand View Restaurant!*"

No one answered.

Hannah went back over to the front door, opened it, and ran inside.

"Hey!" she yelled. "Is anybody home?"

"Come into the kitchen," she heard her mother call. "I have something for you."

Hannah ran into the kitchen.

Her mother was sitting at the table shelling almonds and dropping them into a bowl of raisins.

"Ooh—raisins and almonds!" said Hannah. "I *love* raisins and almonds. Can I have some?"

"Why do you think I'm sitting here with a nut-cracker?" asked her mother. "I don't crack nuts for customers. This is an after-school special. How did you like being a bus rider?"

Hannah popped an almond and two raisins into her mouth.

"Mmm—crunchy and chewy at the same time,"

she said. "Raisins and almonds are my favorite snack. The bus was all right. But it was noisy. And I didn't know anybody on it."

"You'll get to know the children on the bus," said her mother. "And it can't be noisier than those radio programs you listen to every night after supper. Especially *The Lone Ranger.*"

"I love *The Lone Ranger,*" said Hannah, biting into another almond. "I think I'll go exploring now and see what it's like up on the mountain in Grand View." She chewed two more raisins.

"Change your clothes and drink a glass of milk first," said her mother.

"Of course," said Hannah. "Don't I always? I meant *after.*"

Hannah went into her bedroom and changed her clothes.

Back in the kitchen, she poured herself a glass of milk, put a napkin in the center of the table, and sat down. While she drank, she picked out five almonds and put them in the center of the napkin. Then she picked out ten raisins and put them on top of the almonds. Then very carefully she tied the four corners of the napkin together like a little knapsack.

"Thanks for cracking all those almonds," she said to her mother. "I'll finish my snack on the mountain. See you later."

"Cross carefully," said her mother.

Before Hannah left, she went down the outside cement steps on the side of the hill and opened the door to the cellar. Her father was hammering at his worktable. There were two wooden sawhorses nearby with a big saw lying across them. Long pieces of wood and piles of sawdust were all over the floor.

"What are you doing?" Hannah asked her father.

"I'm making a new invention. I've been measuring and sawing all day."

"What are you making?" asked Hannah. "Tell!"

"It's a secret."

"Just tell *me*," said Hannah.

"Then it wouldn't be a secret anymore," said her father. "Anyhow, you should be outside getting fresh air on a beautiful sunshiny day like this."

"I am," said Hannah. "I'm going exploring. See

you later." She closed the door. Then she opened it again. "The sign looks wonderful," she yelled in. "Especially the question marks and periods!" She closed the cellar door again.

As she walked up the outside cellar stairs, her mother was just coming out to her garden on the side of the hill. She had a funny straw hat on her head.

"Your hat looks like an upside-down ice-cream cone!" said Hannah. "Oh—what are those things in your hands? They look like onions! Are you planting onions?"

"You'll see in the spring," said her mother. "My garden will be a surprise—like your father's inventions."

"Well, if you *are* planting onions, we can put them on hamburgers and serve them to customers," said Hannah.

"You'll see," said her mother again. "Now go— do your exploring. I hope you find your same favorite place on the mountain that you like so much."

"I hope so too," said Hannah. "That's what I'm

going to look for. But this road going up isn't the same road I took from our other neighborhood, so what if I can't find it?"

"Well, it's the same mountain, even though we're in Grand View," said Hannah's mother. "There are a few different roads on the mountain, but I think they all join together. Anyhow, that's what exploring is. It's an adventure. Who knows what you'll find."

"Okay," said Hannah. "See you later."

She looked both ways and crossed 9W. Then she took the road that went up the side of the mountain.

"I could sprinkle raisins and almonds along the way," she said to herself, "in case I got lost. Like Hansel and Gretel did with crumbs.

"I don't think I'll do that though." She patted her knapsack. "Raisins and almonds are too good to sprinkle on the ground. I'd rather save them and eat them when I get to the top. *If* I find my special place."

Halfway up the steep road on the side of the mountain, she looked to the right and saw another road that joined it. "That's Shadyside Avenue!" she said. "The road I used to take from our old neighborhood. And right here is where I used to turn and start up this steep road. I know right where I am now—the rest of the way's the same!" She began to run.

When she got to the top of the steep road, she turned left and ran up the last road.

She hurried faster as she got near the top of the mountain.

Finally she got to the very top. She turned and held her breath and crossed her fingers to make sure the beautiful view would still be there.

Everything was there, just the same: the big river, the boats, the mountain on the other side, the houses on the mountain on the other side, the big sky, and the sun sparkling over everything.

Hannah let her breath out. "Hooray! I found it! My special place," she said. "Look at that river *shine!*"

She sat down next to a funny tree that was jutting out sideways from the edge of the mountain. She looked down below her feet. The tops of the trees below her were orange, yellow, and red. Only the needles on the pine trees were still green. She found the roof of her school and now the roof of The Grand View Restaurant. She pictured her mother in the garden on the slope of the hill, planting those things that looked like onions, and she pictured her father in the cellar a little farther down, sawing and hammering on his invention.

She looked across the river and over to her right.

"That's where the Bronx is," she said to herself. "Across the river and a lot of miles over. I wonder what my grandparents are doing."

She looked straight across the river at the other side. She saw the lighthouse. Hannah knew that was Tarrytown. There was a ferry that crossed from Nyack over to Tarrytown. She looked for the ferry and found it. She wondered if the Eskimo Pie man was on it, and the man who played the violin. Thinking about the Eskimo Pie man made her hungry. She opened her knapsack and took out an almond and two raisins. While she chewed and crunched, she watched a barge. It was just to the left of the lighthouse. It hardly seemed to move.

She stared at the mountain on the other side. "I wonder," she thought, "if someone is sitting over there on the mountain looking over here. And suppose somebody *is*—wouldn't it be funny if that person was wondering if someone's over here looking there?"

She looked all around her. "I wonder what I'll be when I grow up," she thought. Hannah wondered about that all the time. She popped another almond and two raisins into her mouth and closed her knapsack.

She chewed as slowly as the could and stared across the river some more. She still wondered if someone was sitting on the other side looking over at her side.

"Yoo hoo, over there if you are!" she yelled. "It's me, Hannah! What are you going to be when *you* grow up?"

Secretly Hannah wanted to be in the movies. She never told that to anybody because she was afraid they would laugh at her. But her grandmother always said she could tap-dance better than Shirley Temple.

Hannah got up and sang "East Side, West Side" and tap-danced to it. She sang "Bye Bye Blackbird" and "Alexander's Ragtime Band" and tap-danced to those too. Then she sat back down.

She looked down at the ground. "I think I'll lie down and look at the sky through the trees," she said. "The leaves can be my mattress." She squinted her eyes and saw light from the sun flash between the dark-green needles of the pine trees. She saw the red, orange, and yellow leaves on the other trees and tried to decide which color leaves were her favorite. When she looked at a tree with red leaves, she thought it was red. But then when she looked at a tree with orange leaves, she thought it was orange. And when she looked at a tree with yellow leaves, she thought it was yellow.

"I can never choose," said Hannah. "I wonder if I'll ever make up my mind about *anything*."

She looked at the blue sky through the

branches. She watched the shapes of the clouds and stared until she saw three in a row that looked like rabbits. "Flopsy, Mopsy, and Cottontail!" she said. "Isn't that amazing—I *always* see someone I know!" She thought of the blackberries and cream Mrs. Rabbit gave them for supper. "Mmm," said Hannah. "I'm hungry again." She sat up and opened her knapsack and took out another almond and two raisins. She closed the knapsack back up and chewed slowly again.

Then she got up and piled a bunch of leaves together and jumped in the middle so she could hear them go crunch. And then she picked up her knapsack and started down the side of the mountain.

On the way down, she began to wonder what it was like down by the river in Grand View. The mountain was the same mountain and the river was still the same river, but when she went down to the river from her neighborhood in Nyack, she came to a park. She wondered what was down by the river in Grand View. So she decided to explore the river too.

She continued straight down the mountain road till she came to 9W again. She looked both ways, crossed, and came to a place where Broadway ended and joined 9W. She walked down Broadway. Soon she came to Cornelison Avenue, where the Nyack bus turned toward the River Road. She walked down Cornelison Avenue. She came to the River Road. After a while, she came to a stretch of sand along the river and walked over onto the sand. She kept walking along the sand till she came to a cove. In the cove was an old tree trunk. Hannah sat down on the tree trunk and looked at the river again. She found the ferry. She found the barge. The barge was just on the right side of the light-house now.

"Boy, barges are really *slow*," she thought.

"I wonder if the person who might be over there on the other side is still looking over here," she thought. She looked over for a long while.

"I'm down by the river now, if you're still there," she called.

She got up and walked on the sand along the

edge of the water. She followed a bird's foot-prints. She found a long curly feather and a shiny silvery stone. She picked them up and went back toward the log and sat down again and examined them. The quill of the feather was white. The hairs were blue-gray with white edges. The silvery stone turned gold when she turned it around and around in the sunlight. "Oh," thought Hannah, "there are so many beautiful things!"

She looked down at the log she was sitting on.

"I wonder who's longer, me or this log," she said to herself. "I'll mea-sure." She lay down on the log with the knapsack, the feather, and the stone on her stomach.

"It's exactly the same length I am!" she thought. "This must be my own private log." She closed her eyes a minute. The sunlight felt warm and good on her face and hair and eye-lids. "My eyebrows are getting toasted!" she said. She picked up the feather, the stone, and the knapsack and got up and looked all around. "It's nice and cozy down here in this cove," she thought. "Now I have a special place down by the river too."

She found a place in the sand near the log where there was a big square made out of birds' footprints. She bent down, and inside the square she wrote with the point of the feather:

THIS IS MY OTHER
SECRET PLACE.
SIGNED,
HANNAH
P.S. DO NOT ERASE THIS!!!

She untied the knapsack and ate two almonds and four raisins. Then she took the feather, the stone, and the napkin and ran up the River Road till she came to Cornelison Avenue. She kept running up Cornelison till she came to Broadway, ran up Broadway till she came to where it joined 9W, and turned and ran more on 9W till she came to:

HUNGRY? THIRSTY?
STOP HERE.
THE GRAND VIEW RESTAURANT.

A car was just driving away from the gas station and Hannah's mother was just putting the nozzle of the hose back into one of the gas pumps.

"I found my special place!" yelled Hannah. "And I found a *new* place too!"

"Good!" said her mother, wiping her hands with a clean rag. "I was just beginning to wonder if you were coming back!"

"Of course," said Hannah. "I had to come back." She waved the napkin at her mother. "I ran out of raisins and almonds."

The New Invention

Hannah's father came running up the outside steps from the cellar. He was carrying a saw, a measuring tape, and a hammer. More things were bulging out of the pockets of a carpenter's apron he was wearing. At the top of the steps he pushed the gate open and hurried around to the front door of the restaurant. His cheeks were pink and his eyes were shining. "My new invention is almost ready," he called as he ran through the doorway.

"It should be something special," said Hannah's mother. "I never heard so much loud banging in my life. I heard you when I was in my garden, and I heard you when I was inside the kitchen cooking hamburgers, and I even heard one loud bang all the way from the gas pumps a minute ago! It sounded like you were knocking the whole place down."

"Wait until you see," said Hannah's father. "It won't be long now. If anyone has to use the bathroom, use it now."

Hannah ran in and out.

"Okay," said Hannah's father. "I'm going in there and don't ask me any questions till I come out.

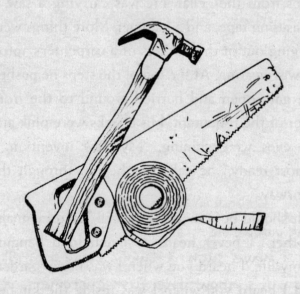

Don't wait for me because I don't know how long it will take."

"I think I'll start supper," said Hannah's mother.

"I think I'll write a letter to Grandma," said Hannah. She went into her room and rolled up the rolltop desk and sat down.

She got a piece of paper and a pencil. She began to write.

Dear Grandma,

I got your homework. It was the first mail that came to The Grand View Restaurant! You got 100% and a gold star. Good work, Trudy! You know your arithmetic!

I was on my special place on the mountain before and I looked across the river and over to the right and I was thinking about you. Were you thinking about me?

I have such a funny thing to tell you. It's about the first customers, a man and a lady. We all wanted to take the order. My father did, my mother did, and I did. We had a race. My father got to their table fastest, so he was first. But my mother and I were right behind him. The man said to my father, "We'd like two eggs, one fried on one side and one fried on the other side." My father wrote it down on a little pad. Then my father and mother went back to the kitchen. So did I. My father looked at the pad. He said to my mother, "How do you fry one egg on one side and one egg on the other side?" She didn't know either. So we all went out to the restaurant to ask. The man and lady laughed and laughed. It was a joke! Wasn't that funny?

Then they ordered two hamburgers and two Coca-Colas. I was the waitress. And I pushed the Coca-Colas through the soda machine. I also pumped "Bye Bye Blackbird" on the player piano while they were eating. And I got a tip—a whole nickel!

I'm making you some more homework.

Love,
Hannah

P.S. I can hardly wait for Halloween, can you? I'm invited to a party!

Hannah took a new sheet of paper with lines out of one of the drawers in her rolltop desk. Slowly she made up ten spelling words. She left a blank in each word. At the top she wrote, "Fill in the blanks." Then she reached into another drawer in the desk and took out her drawing pad. She took out a piece of paper and put the pad back. She took out an empty matchpad with a drawing of a lady's profile. Next to the lady it said, DRAW ME! Hannah drew the lady on the left side of the sheet of paper. Then she wrote, "DRAW ME!" She made a little arrow pointing to the right side of the paper, and in smaller letters she wrote, "OVER HERE." She put the spelling paper on top of the lady and the letter on top of the spelling paper and she folded the letter, the spelling paper, and the lady together. She took an envelope from another cubbyhole. She wrote her grandmother's name and address on the envelope. She folded the three pages two more times until they were the right size to fit into the envelope. Then she licked the flap and pressed it down. She got a three-cent stamp from one of the cubbyholes and licked the stamp and pressed that down neatly in the top right-hand corner of the envelope. In the top left corner of the envelope, she wrote, "From Hannah, The Grand View Restaurant, Grand View, New York."

Then she heard such a loud hammering and sawing from the bathroom, she couldn't wait another minute to find out what the surprise invention was, and she ran out of the bedroom and yelled, *What is it?*"

Hannah's father flung open the bathroom door.

Hannah looked in. "Ooh!" she yelled. "There's a big hole in the bathroom floor!"

Her mother came running.

Hannah and her mother stared at the hole.

"Don't go away!" said Hannah's father. He ran through the living room and kitchen, out the front door of the restaurant, and down the outside steps to the cellar.

Hannah and her mother kept staring at the hole. They looked down and saw the cellar floor. All of a sudden, they saw the top of Hannah's father's head.

He looked up. "Yoo hoo!" he called. "Watch this."

He picked up a ladder. He put it so the bottom of it was on the floor of the cellar and the top of it came up to the edge of the hole in the bathroom floor. "Perfect fit," he said. "I made it just right."

"Now change places with me," he said. "I'm coming up. You two come down."

"Can I come down the ladder?" asked Hannah.

"Not yet," said her father. "I have to attach it first. Come down the outside stairs."

Hannah and her mother went around the

outside and down the stairs to the cellar.

"Your father and his inventions!" said Hannah's mother. "He better close up that hole fast—before somebody falls down and breaks a leg."

Hannah ran into the cellar ahead of her mother.

"I need you two to hold the bottom of the ladder," said Hannah's father. He ran around and up the outside steps again. "This is the last time I use those outside steps," he said.

Hannah and her mother held the bottom of the ladder. They kept staring up at the hole. All of a sudden they saw the tips of Hannah's father's shoes. He looked down.

"Yoo hoo!" he called again. "Now watch this. Just hold the ladder still."

They held the ladder.

Hannah's father banged several long nails through the top of the ladder and into the wooden beams under the bathroom floor.

"Now come back up," he called down. "Use the outside steps, and by the time you get here the hole will be gone!"

When Hannah and her mother got back up,

they heard a very loud bang. "The last one!" said Hannah's father. "Okay—come look."

Hannah and her mother looked into the bathroom.

"The hole *is* gone!" said Hannah. "What did you do?"

"I put the piece I took *out* back *in!*" said her father. "I attached it on one side with hinges. Now watch this." He hammered one more piece of hardware onto the piece of wood that closed the hole, and another into the floor right next to it. "Now take hold of this metal thing and pull up," he said.

Hannah did. There was the hole again. She looked into the cellar.

"Now," said Hannah's father. *"Watch this!"*

He climbed down the wooden ladder and into the cellar.

Hannah looked down and saw her father looking up. "Now we've got an inside stairway!" he said. "Who wants to be next?"

"Oh, can I?" asked Hannah.

"Why not?" said her father.

"Be careful," said her mother.

"Of course!" said Hannah. She went down the steps of the ladder. Her mother followed her.

"I think it should have something on the sides, to hold on to," said her mother.

"Certainly," said Hannah's father. "Railings." He held up two more long pieces of wood. "Now that my stairway is attached to the floor of the bathroom, I can attach my railings to my stairway. Well, ladies, how do you like my latest patent? If I do say so myself, this is some invention. A *trapdoor!* Now when it snows, I won't have to shovel my way down those outside steps."

"It's amazing!" said Hannah.

"What if somebody is in the bathroom and you want to come up the inside stairway?" asked her mother.

"Follow me," said Hannah's father. He walked up his stairway into the bathroom.

Hannah followed her father and her mother followed her.

"It's very steep," said Hannah's mother.

"But when I put my railings up, it'll be fine. Now

watch," said Hannah's father when they were all up and in. He put the trapdoor down. He slid a piece of metal he had attached to the floor next to the trapdoor into a piece of metal he had attached to the trapdoor next to it. "This is a slide bolt," he said. "If you come into the bathroom, the first thing you do is slide it across and lock it. Then if I come up, it won't open and I'll know to wait. When you go out of the bathroom, slide it back and unlock it. When it's unlocked, I can come up."

"What an invention!" said Hannah.

"You said it!" said her father. "If I do say so myself. Now I'll go down and attach the railings."

"Can I help?" asked Hannah.

"Okay," said her father. "You can hold on while I'm nailing so it doesn't move."

"I want to nail one nail in too," said Hannah. "On each side. Like I nailed in the question marks and periods on the sign."

"Follow me," said her father.

"Can I have a soda with supper to celebrate the new invention?" Hannah asked her mother.

"Soda fills you up too much," said Hannah's

mother. "Oh—all right. You can have half with your supper and half after."

"I think I'll have Orange Crush this time," said Hannah. She watched her father open the trapdoor. She turned around. "Or maybe grape," she said. She followed her father down the inside steps.

"Wait a minute!" she told him when she got to the bottom.

She ran back up the stairs. She pushed the trapdoor open. "Ma!" she called.

Her mother came over. "What is it?" she asked.

"Sarsaparilla!" said Hannah.

Home-safe

Hannah snapped off the light on the table next to her bed and slid in underneath the feather quilt. Everything felt so familiar now. She felt like she had been here always.

"Mmm," she said, curling her toes. "It feels so cozy."

She turned to the wall next to the bed and studied the leaf shadows in the moonlight.

"I could be an artist," she said to herself, "when I grow up. In case I can't be in the movies."

She rolled over and put the light back on and looked at the clock on her dresser.

"I've got lots of time," she said.

She got out of bed and went over to her desk.

She rolled the top up and sat down. She opened the drawer with her drawing pad in it, took out a piece of paper, and put the pad back in the drawer.

Then she drew the lady on the matchpad without even taking the matchpad out of its cubbyhole.

"DRAW ME!" she wrote next to the picture. She took the matchpad out of the cubbyhole under the rolltop and put it next to her picture. "It looks *just* like it," she said.

She took out her box of crayons with forty-eight colors and gave her lady a hat with curly feathers and a fur scarf with a fox's nose at the end.

She took the drawing pad back out and put the picture inside it, right on top of a drawing of the funny old sideways tree at the top of the mountain. "I drew that from memory too," she thought. She put the drawing pad away.

She opened another drawer and felt underneath the pile of paper with lines on it till she felt something smooth and hard.

She slid out a pepper-and-salt notebook. On the front of the notebook, in the middle of the black-and-white speckles, was a little white rectangle. In the middle of the little white rectangle it said, in capital letters:

HANNAH'S SECRET THINGS.
DO NOT OPEN THIS BOOK!!!

Hannah opened the notebook and turned the pages. On the first page it said, "I earned the nickel to buy this new pepper-and-salt all by myself. Signed, Hannah."

On the second page it said, "Things I Like," and on the third page, "Things I Don't Like." The fourth page said, "Things I Wish." Hannah turned to the fifth page, where it said, "Things I Might Be When I Grow Up." The first line said, "I might be a waitress." The second line said, "I might be a movie star." On the third line, Hannah wrote, "I might be an artist."

She turned back to page four, "Things I Wish," and wrote, "I wish I could make up my mind."

She closed the book and slid it back in the drawer underneath the pile of paper with lines. Then she closed the drawer and looked around at the rest of the room.

"This room is beautiful!" she said. "I love everything in it!"

She looked at the clock again. "I've still got time," she thought. She opened the drawer and took the pepper-and-salt back out. She turned to "Things I Like" and wrote:

"I like my new bed. My mother took me to Brown's Furniture and we picked it out together. It has four posts with a pineapple carved out on top of each one. So I call it my pineapple bed."

Hannah drew a picture of her bed. Then she wrote:

"I like my new wallpaper. I picked it out all by myself from a book Aggie Branagan's father had in his truck. It's white with tiny pink roses and green leaves."

She drew a picture of a truck and lettered on the side of it "BRANAGAN'S PAINTING AND

PAPERING. CHEAP." She drew a picture of the wallpaper pattern and colored in the flowers and leaves. Then she wrote:

"I like my whole room because it has pineapples and roses." She got up and put her hand on the wallpaper and felt the bumps.

She went back to her desk and turned to the page that said, "Things I Wish," and wrote, "I wish my mother didn't get so mad at Mr. Branagan just because he left a lot of lumps of paste under the wallpaper."

She turned back to "Things I Like" and wrote, "I still like Mr. Branagan."

She looked out the window and saw the tree in her mother's garden. She turned to the page that said, "Things I Don't Like," and wrote:

"I hate that ugly little tree in my mother's garden. It turned out to be a *sumac* tree and it gave my mother poison sumac on her hands. Her hands got so itchy and sore she had to go to the doctor. My father tried to pull the tree out but the roots were too long."

Hannah took a little memo pad out of one of the cubbyholes, tore off the top piece of paper, and wrote,

Dear Ma,

Don't go out there in your garden anymore. I feel terrible when I look at your hands.

Love,
Hannah

P.S. I think the lumps under the wallpaper make the roses look more real.

She folded the note in half. Then she took it and went out into the living room.

There was soft music coming from the radio. Her father was sitting by a lamp reading *The New York Times*. On the floor next to his feet, Hannah saw the *New York Herald Tribune*.

Her mother was sitting near another lamp. There was a book on the table next to her, and next to the book was a little bottle. She was dabbing pink lotion from the bottle onto her hands with a piece of cotton.

"Is that the stuff the doctor gave you?" asked Hannah.

"Yes," said her mother. "Calamine lotion. To keep it from spreading. He said I should use brown soap and alcohol after gardening for prevention. And this is to use if I get it anyhow."

"But if you don't make a garden there, you won't get it at all," said Hannah.

"I have to garden there," said Hannah's mother. "There's no place else."

"So don't have a garden."

"I have to have a garden."

"But *why?*"

"I'll tell you another time when it's not bedtime," said Hannah's mother. "What are you doing out of bed, anyway?"

"I was writing things and drawing things," said Hannah. "Here's a note for you." She put the note on the table on top of her mother's book.

"Good-bye," she said. "I have to hurry."

"What's the hurry?" asked her father.

"I don't want to miss my train," said Hannah. She kissed her parents good night again and went back to her room.

She looked at the clock on her dresser. "It's almost time!" she said.

The pages in her notebook had flipped over. She opened it up to page two, "Things I Like," and wrote:

"When the train comes by at night. I always wait for it—ever since we moved here. I make believe I've been away on a trip and I'm coming back home. Just like the people on the train."

Hannah closed the pepper-and-salt notebook and put it away. She put the memo pad back in its cubbyhole and gave a quick good-night pat to all the secret things in the other cubbies: the stone, the shell, the feather, a tiny rubber ball, some jacks, some glass marbles with pretty colors running together inside. Then she rolled down the top of her desk, snapped the light off, slid in under her feather quilt, and turned back to the wall next to the bed.

She studied the leaf shadows some more. They were very still; nothing moved. "The shadow looks glued on," thought Hannah. "Like a picture pasted to the wall!" At night, outlined on the wall, the tree didn't look as ugly as in the daytime.

"But I still hate that tree!" she thought. "I wish I could pull it out by the roots myself!"

Suddenly the leaf shadows began to rustle and whisper and move, and Hannah began to hear the sound.

"I can hear it!" she said. "It's down at the crossing. It's almost here!" She held her breath.

She listened and watched. The sound got louder. The shadows of the leaves began a wild dance over the wall. Then everything began to jump and jiggle: all the little secret things inside the cubbyholes in the rolltop desk, the clock on top of the dresser, the lamp on the table next to the bed, and the bed itself, with Hannah in it. She kept holding her breath and listening and watching until the shadows moved slower, the shaking stopped, and everything got quiet.

Then Hannah felt like she would explode, so she let her breath out. She pulled the feather quilt up to her nose and closed her eyes. She felt the moonlight bright on her face. She could feel it settling white and cool across her eyelids.

"Home-safe!" she whispered into the quilt.

She heard one little faraway toot and then she fell asleep.

Halloween on the Mountain

Hannah stood outside with a sheet over her head. She looked out through two holes. "Boo!" she said, flapping her arms. "I'm a ghost!"

She looked up at the mountain. "It's getting dark!" she thought. "Soon I'll be up there!" She flapped her arms and danced in a circle. Then she looked over at the gasoline station. A light was on inside the garage. She went over and looked inside the big window. Her father was at his roll-top desk in the corner, writing. "Boo!" she said. Her father kept on writing.

Hannah went over to the door of the garage, opened it, and ran inside. She waved her arms at her father and danced around the desk. Her father kept writing.

"Hey!" said Hannah. "I'm a ghost!" Her father's head bent lower.

"It's almost dark," said Hannah. "Almost time to take me to Aggie's."

"Just as soon as I finish my letter to *The New York Times*," said her father. "Only a few more minutes. I don't want to lose my thoughts."

"Okay," said Hannah, "but I told Aggie I'd come as soon as it's dark." She ran back to the restaurant.

"Daddy's writing a letter to the editor again," she said to her mother. "Oh—I can't wait."

Her mother held out a brown paper bag and a sweater. "Here," she said, "one of Aunt Becky's nice warm sweaters to put on under your sheet."

"Ugh!" said Hannah. "I was hoping you'd forget about a sweater."

"Lift your arms," said her mother. "I'll help you put it on under the sheet."

"I'll be the only one who has to wear a sweater on Halloween," said Hannah. "I'll be itchy. Aunt

Becky knits with itchy wool."

"Aunt Becky gets the warmest wool there is," said Hannah's mother. "On Halloween it gets cool at night. Especially up there on the mountain."

Hannah lifted her arms. Her mother helped her get the sweater on. They both looked up at the big dark mountain.

"Are you sure you want to go up there?" asked her mother. "Why don't you just go up and down the street with Aggie and the others the way you used to?"

"I'm not a baby anymore," said Hannah. "We all crossed 9W and went on the mountain last year. It's the best place I ever went to on Halloween. That old man and lady in the house on the road near the top made us a party!"

"Didn't Miss Pepper make you a party in school this afternoon?"

"Yes, but school parties don't count. All we got to eat was Necco wafers and candy corn—and Miss Pepper made us do arithmetic with them first! I don't even *like* Necco wafers and candy corn; I'd rather have one of those licorice or cherry cough drops Miss Pepper keeps in her desk, but she never gives those to anybody except when they're monitor. Last Halloween the man and lady on the mountain had all the good things I like—and they invited us in for a party. We bobbed for apples and told ghost stories! They said come again next year and we promised. You always say people should keep their promises. Besides, I've been waiting all year."

"But it looks so dark up there," said Hannah's mother.

"It *is* dark," said Hannah. "That's why it's so good. You can scare each other better in the dark. Don't worry, I'm not going alone." She looked at the big dark mountain and pictured herself going alone. Hannah didn't like being in the dark by herself. Underneath her sheet she shivered, even with Aunt Becky's woolly sweater.

"Well, stick close together," said Hannah's mother. "Call us when you're ready to come home."

"Okay," said Hannah. She heard the car horn. "Oh—Daddy's finished with his letter! Hooray!"

"Have a good time then," said her mother.

"I will," said Hannah. "Oh, I can't wait for the party!" She took her brown paper bag and got into the car.

"Wow—it's really dark now," she said to her father. "Boo! I'm a ghost! Take me to Aggie's house."

Her father drove slowly. Hannah saw ghosts and goblins running in little groups along the way.

"Almost everybody's a ghost, like me," she said.

"Almost everybody has old sheets," said her father.

"I wish you could see the house where we're invited," said Hannah. "They have a real fireplace. And they made a real fire in it. It was beautiful. I hope we have another one."

"I *would* love a house with a fireplace in it," said Hannah's father. "If I had one, at the end of the day I'd read all my papers, then I'd make a fire and turn off all the lights and just sit back and stare at it. Well, I can't afford a house with a fireplace. But

I'm working on a new idea for something else I can just sit and stare at instead. This will be nice too."

"Oh, you're making a new invention," said Hannah. "What is it?"

"I can't tell you," said her father.

"Why not?"

"Because look where we are!"

Hannah looked out the window and saw three ghosts dancing around on the sidewalk.

"We're here!" she said.

The three ghosts came running over to the car as Hannah started to get out.

"Boo!" they yelled. "We're ghosts!"

"Boo yourself, Aggie, Otto, and Frankie!" Hannah yelled back. "You can't scare me! I'm a ghost too!"

"Call when you're ready to come home, Ghost," said Hannah's father.

"I will," said Hannah. She closed the car door and her father drove on.

"Aggie!" said Hannah to the shortest ghost. "Just wait till that man and lady see us again.

They'll say, 'Here are the four ghosts we've been waiting for all year.' Will they be glad to see us! I'll bet they've been waiting for Halloween too, just the way we have."

"We're going to town first," said Otto.

"*Town?*" said Hannah. "What do you mean, *town?* We're going up on the mountain."

"We're going up on the mountain *after,*" said Otto. "First we're going to town. Willie Hoffman told me he went to town last year and he went in all the doctors' offices. They gave him *money.*"

"The man and lady on the mountain gave us money too, Otto," said Hannah. "Besides all the other stuff they gave us and the party, they gave us each two cents. Don't you remember?"

"Two cents!" said Otto. "Hah! The three doctors in town gave Willie a nickel. *Each!*"

"Three nickels!" said Frankie.

"That's fifteen cents, Hannah," said Aggie.

"Oh, Aggie," said Hannah. "They're waiting for us. We promised."

"We're going to town first," said Otto. "*Then* the mountain."

"How come you always think you're the boss of everything, Otto?" asked Hannah. "All year long we said we're going back on the mountain for Halloween. And today in school just before I got back on the bus, we even all said we were going on the mountain."

"But after you got on the bus, when we walked home, Willie Hoffman was walking with us till he got to his street, and he told us about the three nickels he got last year. And that's when I decided we're going to town."

"But how come you decided? How come you're the boss?"

"Because I just am," said Otto. "That's how come." He started walking down the street. Frankie followed him.

"Aggie," said Hannah. "Are we going to let Otto be the boss of us?"

"Let's go make Otto promise to go up on the mountain as soon as we get back from town," said Aggie.

"But why do you want to go to town at all, Aggie?" asked Hannah. "I'll bet they're making the fire up there already. We should go *now.*"

"Hannah, I'm afraid to go up on the dark mountain with just the two of us," said Aggie. "I'd be too scared."

"Otto and Frankie kept coming up behind us and saying 'Boo!' all the way up the mountain last year," said Hannah. "They scared us all the way up and all the way down, so what's the difference? Let's go without them."

"Oh, I don't know, Hannah; I don't know what to do," said Aggie. "Let's go and ask Otto if we can run to town and back. Fifteen cents is so much money. Then we can run up the mountain too." Aggie began to run down the street after Otto and Frankie.

"Hey, wait up!" said Aggie.

"Boo!" yelled Otto and Frankie, turning around and flapping their arms.

Hannah ran down after Aggie. "It's not fair!" she said. "Money isn't everything. We *promised!*"

"Boo!" said Otto.

"You can't scare me on the street, Otto," said Hannah. "Because there are lights. And in town, there'll be more lights, so you can't scare me in town either. Nobody can scare me anyplace on Halloween except on the mountain. Besides, that man and lady are waiting for us up there. You should never break a promise."

"Why don't you go up alone if you're in such a hurry?" asked Otto.

"Oh, you *Otto!*" said Hannah. "That's not fair!" Hannah wished she *could* go up on the mountain alone. But when she pictured herself alone on the big dark mountain, she got goose pimples all over her skin. "I can't stand you, Otto," she said to herself.

"Otto, promise," said Aggie. "Promise we'll go up on the mountain as soon as we get back from town. And promise we'll go fast."

"I promise, I promise!" said Otto. "Come on, *run!* That's how fast we'll go. Last one down to the bottom of the street is a rotten egg!"

The four ghosts ran down the street, as fast as they could run.

When they got to Broadway, they turned left and began to run toward town.

They saw other little groups of ghosts and goblins going up to the doors of the houses on both sides of the street along Broadway.

Otto and Frankie followed one group onto the front porch of a house.

"This isn't town, Otto," said Hannah, running up on the porch. "You said we'd run to town, run back, and go up on the mountain before it gets too late."

"Well, we might as well get stuff from the houses along the way," said Otto.

"Otto, you *said!*" said Hannah.

The door opened and a lady looked out.

"Why, look at those four ghosts," said the lady. "I'll bet they'd like some candy corn."

Otto, Frankie, and Aggie opened their bags.

"I hate candy corn," Hannah whispered to Aggie.

"Take it and give it to me," Aggie whispered back.

Hannah opened her bag too and the lady dropped in a handful of candy corn.

"Thank you," said Hannah. As soon as the door

closed, Hannah opened her bag, scooped the candy corn out, and gave it to Aggie.

"Thanks, Hannah," said Aggie. She was eating some of hers already. "I just love candy corn."

They ran on.

Otto and Frankie stopped at all the houses along the way. Aggie followed. Hannah was last. She kept saying, *"Hurry up!"*

Almost everyone gave out candy corn, apples, or Necco wafers. Hannah kept the apples, but she gave all her candy corn and Necco wafers to Aggie.

"I hate those," she said.

"I love them," said Aggie through a mouthful.

Finally they got to town. They went to the three doctors Willie Hoffman got nickels from last year, and they each got nickels too.

"Three nickels!" said Aggie, with her mouth full of Necco wafers and candy corn. "Fifteen cents!"

"I told you!" said Otto.

"This isn't any fun, though," said Hannah. "They don't talk to you like the man and lady. They gave us nickels just to get rid of us. There

are so many streetlights and houses here, it's not scary a bit. Now let's hurry back so we can go up on the mountain. Let's run! Aggie, what's taking you so long? Let's go faster."

Aggie was rummaging around in her bag. "I just can't stop eating the candy corn and Necco wafers," she said.

"Save some for tomorrow," said Hannah, "or tomorrow you'll wish you still had them and you'll be sorry. Besides, we have to hurry. Run!"

Hannah began to run. Otto, Frankie, and Aggie ran after her.

"Hey, slow down, Hannah!" said Otto.

"I can't run so fast," said Aggie.

"But they're waiting for us," said Hannah. "With the *party*. They're probably wondering what happened to us. Maybe they'll think we're not coming. Maybe the fire will be out!" She kept running.

"Hannah," called Aggie. "Stop! Wait a minute. I don't feel so good. I can't run."

Hannah stopped running and turned around.

"Oh, Aggie—what's the matter?" she asked.

"I have a bellyache," said Aggie.

"A *bellyache!*" said Hannah. She hated to even hear that word. "Oh, no! Not on Halloween just when we're going to go up on the mountain."

"Hannah," said Aggie, "I can't go. I have to go home and lie down."

"Yay!" yelled Otto.

"What do you mean 'yay'?" said Hannah. "Aggie has a bellyache. The man and lady on the mountain are waiting for us. We promised we'd come again. This is *terrible!* What do you mean 'yay'?"

"I've got a whole bag of candy and three nickels," said Otto. "And I don't *feel* like going up on the mountain. There's not enough houses there to bother with. I'm going to go home and eat my candy."

"You promised!" said Hannah. "We can walk Aggie home and then still go up."

"Well, I don't feel like it," said Otto. "And I'm not going." They were still walking while they were talking. They came to their street and turned up it.

"Oh, Hannah," said Aggie, "I'm sorry."

"You can't help it if you got a bellyache," said Hannah. "I'll walk you to your door. But if Otto and Frankie don't come, they're stinkers."

"Raspberries!" said Otto. He stuck out his tongue and made a rude noise.

They came to Frankie's house. "Well, I have to go in now," said Frankie. Otto crossed the street to his house, turned around, made a loud raspberry sound again, and went into his house.

"Oh, Hannah, what'll we do?" said Aggie. "I think I have to throw up."

"Wait, here's your house," said Hannah. She helped Aggie up the front stoop to her door.

"Want to come in and call your father?" asked Aggie.

"No, you go in," said Hannah. "I'll stay out here till I figure out what to do. I'm sorry you feel like throwing up, Aggie. I hope you feel better."

Aggie ran into her house.

Hannah went back down the steps onto the sidewalk and looked around.

Some bigger kids were going down the street.

She looked up at Route 9W and across the

street at the big dark mountain. She pictured the old man and lady. In her picture, she saw them opening the front door, looking around, then closing it.

"Well, I guess they're not coming," she imagined the man saying.

"I'm so disappointed," she could picture the lady answering.

She pictured them bobbing for apples all by themselves and telling ghost stories just to each other.

Suddenly Hannah knew what she was going to do.

She closed her eyes a minute and held her breath. Then she opened her eyes and exhaled loudly.

She walked up to Route 9W, adjusted her sheet so she could see better through the holes, looked both ways, and crossed over.

She walked to where Shadyside Avenue started and began walking up, alone. There were some houses on Shadyside. Last year, Hannah, Aggie, Otto, and Frankie had stopped at all of them. But this time Hannah was in a hurry. She was late. Also she was scared. And she was cold—even with Aunt Becky's sweater. So she didn't stop at any of the houses. She just walked as fast as she could. She saw a couple of other Halloweeners coming down Shadyside. They were much bigger than Hannah.

"Boo, little ghost!" said one of them.

Hannah shook and held on to her bag. The big ghost came closer and flapped his arms. "I said, 'Boo, little ghost'" he said.

Hannah adjusted her sheet and looked out and up through the eyeholes. She could see the big ghost's eyes glitter through the eyeholes in *his* sheet.

"He reminds me of Otto," she thought. She looked straight into his eyes.

"Boo yourself, Big Ghost!" she said out loud. "And mind your own business," she whispered under her sheet.

She hurried up Shadyside Avenue. She was glad the big kids were going down.

Soon she came to the end of Shadyside and

turned right. "This is the steep road I take when I come up on the mountain from Grand View," she said to herself. "There are only two houses on this road. The first one is the one with the big apple orchard behind it. The second one's the one with a tree house." She saw the shadowy outlines of the orchard and the tree house.

"I'm glad I have a sheet over my head," thought Hannah. "It's scary being alone in the dark on the mountain. This way I can't see as much." She felt like she was hiding inside the sheet. She had to keep stopping to adjust the holes over her eyes. There were no more streetlights, and it was hard to see.

Suddenly something rubbed against one of Hannah's ankles and she screamed.

"Meow!"

"Oh, it's a *cat*!" said Hannah. "I'm sorry, cat. I didn't mean to scare you. I'm all alone and it's so dark!" The cat arched its back, stuck its tail up straight, and ran away.

Hannah ran on. When she got to the top of the steep road, she looked to the left. "If I turned here, I'd come to my special secret place," she thought. "That's at the very top of the mountain and it would be the scariest of all. There's not even *one* house there!" She turned right instead, where she knew the little house was. She ran as fast as she could until she came to it. Sure enough, there was a light on outside the front door.

"They *are* waiting," said Hannah. "They're waiting for me!"

She ran up and knocked at the door.

"Here I am!" she said, all out of breath, when the door opened. "I made it!"

"One little ghost, all *alone?*" asked the man. "We were expecting four."

"Aggie got a bellyache and Otto and Frankie went back home," said Hannah.

"Oh, come in," said the lady. "You walked all the way up here in the dark by yourself?"

"It was a promise!" said Hannah. She ran inside.

A fire was burning brightly in the fireplace. Hannah could hear the logs crackling. "Come warm yourself," said the lady. Hannah went over and stood close to the fireplace.

"It feels good," she said. "Nice and warm."

The man made cocoa and put a marshmallow in it, just the way Hannah liked. He set it down on a low table in front of the sofa, facing the fire. Hannah looked at the table. She saw a bowl of black, orange, and yellow gumdrops, another bowl of black, orange, and yellow jellybeans, a third bowl of sticky popcorn balls, and two platters, one with doughnuts, and one with licorice sticks.

"All my Halloween favorites!" said Hannah. "Just like last year."

"Help yourself," said the lady, motioning toward the sofa. She helped Hannah take off her sheet.

Hannah sat down. She put her brown paper bag on the floor next to her. Then she had a doughnut with her cocoa. In between bites, she had one black, orange, or yellow gumdrop, one black, orange, or yellow jellybean, and one bite of sticky popcorn ball. She chewed very slowly, to make everything last longer. She swung her feet. She watched the fire and listened to the sounds.

For dessert, she ate the marshmallow at the bottom of her cup and one licorice stick.

"Mmm," said Hannah, licking her fingers, "that's the best Halloween party I ever ate!"

"And all the leftovers are yours to take home," said the lady. She emptied the bowls and platters into Hannah's brown paper bag.

"I'll give Aggie some when her bellyache goes away," said Hannah.

"But you must keep the rest," said the lady. "And here are the nickels."

"*Nickels?*" asked Hannah. "Last year we had pennies!"

"No one else came but the four of you last year. So I had four nickels ready for tonight. You may have them all."

"But that's twenty cents!"

"You're good in arithmetic," said the man.

"Usually I'm terrible in arithmetic," said Hannah. "But I'm the best speller in my class. I'll give one nickel to Aggie. I'll still have fifteen cents. And I got fifteen cents in town. I'll have *thirty cents* all together—oh, wait till Otto hears! Will he be sorry!"

They told each other ghost stories.

They bobbed for apples.

The lady played a Halloween song on the piano and taught the words to Hannah and the man. Then all three of them sang it together.

"We have a piano now too," said Hannah. "We moved to Grand View. We have The Grand View Restaurant."

"We'll have to come down sometime," said the man.

"We have a player piano," said Hannah. "I pump rolls—'Bye Bye Blackbird' and 'Alexander's Ragtime Band.' And my mother just bought the 'Blue Danube.' And as soon as we can find a piano teacher, I'm going to take lessons and learn to play by myself."

"I can give you lessons," said the lady.

"You *can?*"

"Certainly. If you don't mind coming all the way up here high on the mountain once a week."

"I come up on the mountain every day," said Hannah. "I go even higher. I have a special secret place."

"I won't ask you where," said the lady, "because I know special secret places are *very* secret. But once a week, if you come here, I will give you lessons."

"How much is it, please?" asked Hannah. "I'll tell my mother."

"No charge," said the lady. "I'm retired now."

"*Free* piano lessons?" asked Hannah.

"She gives me free lessons all the time," said the man, "since I'm retired too. Maybe you and I could learn a duet."

"Oh, I have to go now!" said Hannah. "I have to run down and tell my mother!" She put her sheet back on and adjusted the eyeholes. She picked up her brown paper bag.

"Would you like us to drive you down?" asked the man. "It must be scary walking alone on the dark mountain."

"It is scary," said Hannah. "But no thanks—I kind of *like* to scare myself on Halloween."

"Then I'll see you next Friday after school," said the lady. "How will that be?"

"Wonderful!" said Hannah. "Friday will be wonderful!"

She ran out and closed the door. Then she knocked at the door, opened it, and called in, "Thank you for the party. It was the best Halloween party I ever went to. My bag is so full of stuff, I'll take some in my lunchbag every day this week. And I'm *rich*."

She closed the door again and ran to the place where she would turn down to go back home. She looked up at the road that would take her even farther up, to her special secret place. She kept looking up. She closed her eyes and held her breath again. Then she opened her eyes and exhaled loudly.

"*I* am the boss of *me*," she said. And suddenly, unexpectedly, she began to run up the last and highest road on the mountain, to her special secret place. She wanted to know what it looked like in the dark.

"I'm running all alone to the top of the mountain at night on Halloween!" she yelled. She had goose pimples on her skin all the way, but she kept on running.

When she got there, to the very top, she turned left. "I'm so glad I have this sheet over my head!" she said to herself.

Then she saw the river and the sky in the dark for the first time in her life, and she gasped.

"Oh, everything *sparkles* so!" she said.

The moon looked like a white Necco wafer with a light inside. The whole river glittered with moonlight. Across the river on the other side, there were tiny pinpoints of light from the houses on the Tarrytown side. The lighthouse had a bigger light that made a shiny ribbon of light all the way across the water, and a beam of light that moved all over the sky.

Hannah got another kind of goose pimples.

"The night is beautiful!" she said. She set down her bag and pulled off her sheet so she could see better. She stood and looked for a long while, watching the moonlight touch all the things that

were so familiar to her in the day. She was very quiet. Then she remembered the day she was up here when she wondered if someone was on the other side looking over at her side.

"Yoo hoo!" she yelled. "Are you there again? It's me, Hannah, and I'm alone in the *dark*—and I'm hardly even scared!"

Then she heard a toot as the night train passed by down below. She pictured the leaf shadows dancing all over the wall next to her bed, and everything shaking and jiggling in her room.

"I'm ready to come home now!" she yelled.

She put her sheet back on and adjusted the eyes so she could see out. She picked up her bag and ran down the mountain as fast as she could go, yelling, "Boo! *Boo! BOO!*" all the way. She ran straight down the steep road till she came to Route 9W in Grand View. She looked both ways, then crossed and ran toward the big sign on the roof that said:

HUNGRY? THIRSTY?

STOP HERE.

THE GRAND VIEW RESTAURANT.

There was a light on the roof, next to the sign. Hannah knew it was lit for her and not for customers.

She ran toward the light and the sign.

Then she opened the front door, ran in, and yelled, "Boo! I'm home!"

Her parents came running out into the restaurant.

"Where *were* you so long?" asked her mother. "You were supposed to call when you were ready to come home."

"I did call," said Hannah. "I called, 'I'm ready to come home now' from the top of the mountain just before I began running down. Didn't you hear me? I was all alone."

"You went up on that dark mountain by yourself?" asked Hannah's mother. "I can't believe you did that. Most times you won't even walk as far as the bathroom in the dark."

"Aggie got sick and Otto and Frankie were stinkers," said Hannah. "And I'm going to get free piano lessons starting on Friday!"

"You're what? From whom?" asked her mother.

"From the lady on the mountain who made the

Halloween party! She used to give lessons. And she said if I come every Friday . . . Oh, am I tired!"

"You can tell us the rest tomorrow," said her mother. She helped Hannah off with her sheet.

Hannah kissed her parents good night, took her bag into her bedroom, got undressed and into her pajamas, used the bathroom, and got into bed. "Oh—the sheets are *cold!*" she called. Her bedroom window was wide open. Hannah got up and closed it.

"Fresh air is healthy!" her father called in.

Her mother came in and slipped a hot-water bottle under the quilt next to Hannah's feet. "Your father and his fresh air!" she said.

"Ah, that feels good," said Hannah. "Thank you."

She pulled the feather quilt up to her chin, and looked at the leaf shadows on her wall.

"Wait till Otto finds out . . ." she murmured. "Mmm—my feet feel so nice and warm. . . ."

She curled her toes around the edge of the hot-water bottle. She fell asleep.

And she dreamed about the beautiful dark but sparkling night and the mountain and the river.

The Hole in the Wall

Hannah sat on the piano bench in the living room and looked at the big hole her father had sawed in the wall next to the piano.

"What in the world is going to fit in there?" she wondered. She stuck her head through and looked at all five tables in the restaurant. Her mother was putting new bottles of ketchup and mustard on the tables.

"Finished practicing your scales?" asked her mother.

"Almost," said Hannah. "I'm still trying to figure out what this big hole is for. It's *so* big, customers could climb through into the living room! I wish Daddy would tell me the secret."

"You know your father," said Hannah's mother. "He loves to make surprises."

"I know," said Hannah, looking up at the big picture on the wall next to the hole. "I liked when he went to New York City last week and brought back this picture from Macy's for a surprise."

Hannah's mother went from the restaurant through the kitchen and into the living room. She looked at the picture with Hannah. It showed a man crossing a bridge. He was looking at a waterfall.

"That surprise was expensive," said Hannah's mother.

Just then the trapdoor in the bathroom opened and shut and Hannah's father walked into the living room.

"What surprise was expensive?" he asked.

"The picture from Macy's," said Hannah's mother.

"I love that picture," said Hannah. "I can't stop looking at it. There are all rainbow colors in the waterfall."

"That's why I bought it," said Hannah's father.

"Now all we have to do is go to Brown's Furniture again and get a new living-room set. Then the place will really be fixed up nice."

"We can't afford to spend so much money," said Hannah's mother.

"But we're saving by not having to pay rent for rooms," said Hannah's father. "Besides, you said you like a place that looks cheerful."

"I also like a place that has privacy, not a big hole in the wall where people can look into my living room."

"It will have privacy, just as soon as I finish my surprise. Don't worry."

"I think it's getting *very* cheerful-looking around here," said Hannah. "But what's the big hole in the wall for? *Tell!*"

"You'll find out soon," said Hannah's father. He took out a tape measure and did some measuring around the edges of the hole.

"We're learning measuring in school," said Hannah. "Miss Pepper gave us each a ruler. But you measured already before you sawed the hole."

"Check and doublecheck." Hannah's father went over to the other end of the living room and looked out through the French doors that didn't go anyplace.

"Look at that snow coming down on top of last week's snow," he said. "We'll be shoveling again tomorrow. When you work in the cellar, you don't even know what's happening outside with the weather. Lucky I have my trapdoor, so I don't have to go in and out by the outside stairs."

"New snow!" said Hannah. "I didn't even know it!" She jumped up and ran over to the French doors too.

"You must have been enjoying your practicing," said her father.

"I hate practicing," said Hannah. "All I do is play scales. I want to play pieces—like the rolls do."

"You have to learn scales before you can play pieces," said her mother.

"I know," said Hannah. "That's what my piano teacher tells me every time I go for a lesson. But I still can't wait to play pieces."

Hannah's father went back down to the cellar through the trapdoor. Her mother went back into the restaurant through the kitchen.

Hannah looked at the clock. "I have to practice ten minutes more," she said. She sat back down on the piano stool.

"Finish practicing, Hannah," her mother said.

"Okay," Hannah answered. "But I still wish I could play the 'Blue Danube' by myself without having to learn scales first."

Just as she started her scales, she got an idea. She took a roll out of the piano bench, opened the two sliding doors over the keyboard, put the paper roll inside, and closed the sliding doors.

"I'll play a little joke on my mother," she said to herself. "As soon as I finish my last scale, I'll start pumping the player piano fast, and she'll think I'm playing a real piece all by myself." Hannah played more scales.

When she was almost finished, her father came up again. He was carrying a hammer and nails and several pieces of wood.

"What's that?" asked Hannah.

"Molding, to put around the edges of the hole," said her father, "so it will be smooth around the edges." He walked through the kitchen and into the restaurant. Then he began to hammer the molding into place. Hannah watched her father and mother through the hole.

"Keep practicing, Hannah," said her mother.

"I have just one more set of scales," said Hannah. "But I'd like to hammer one nail in first."

Her father came back into the living room and nailed the molding around the edges of the hole on that side of the wall.

"Now it'll be smooth on both sides," he said. "Here's the last nail." He handed the hammer to Hannah and she hammered the nail in.

"The molding looks just like a picture frame," she said.

"A picture frame around an empty hole," said her mother.

"It won't be an empty hole for long," said Hannah's father. "I have to get a couple of things from town now. I won't be long."

"You're going to town?" asked Hannah's mother. "Bring hamburger rolls. We're running out."

Hannah's father put on a jacket, got into the car, and drove off.

Hannah had one more set of scales. As she was playing them, the door to the restaurant opened and a bunch of people came in all together. She could see and hear them through the hole in the wall.

They were wearing bright-colored woollen hats and scarves and mittens and heavy sweaters with turtlenecks. They stamped their feet and clapped their hands together.

"Brrr, it's really cold out," one of them said to Hannah's mother. They kept their heavy sweaters on.

"I didn't expect to see any customers today," said Hannah's mother.

"Oh, we're skiers," said one of the people. "We're on our way to Bear Mountain. We love this weather. But we're *hungry*!"

Hannah jumped up to ask her mother if she could take their orders.

"Finish practicing first," said her mother. "I'll take their orders. You can help serve when you're finished."

Hannah didn't like to practice with strangers hearing her, but she liked to wait on tables. She heard them order a lot of hamburgers, and frankfurters, French fries, and cups of coffee. Two of them ordered Coca-Cola, and Hannah wanted to push the sodas through the soda box. So she played her last set of scales fast.

"Remember practicing piano?" she heard one skier ask.

"It sounds very familiar," said another.

"Do re mi fa sol la ti do!" sang a third skier.

Hannah finished.

She was just about to get up and go into the kitchen to ask her mother if she could help. Then she remembered the roll she had put inside the sliding doors over the keyboard.

"They think all I can play is scales," she said to herself.

She began to pump the piano. She pushed the button that made the keys go up and down. She moved her hands up and down the keyboard as the "Blue Danube" began to come out.

"Hey, listen to that!" said one of the skiers. "Classical music! The 'Blue Danube Waltz.'"

Two of them jumped up and began to waltz around the floor in the restaurant.

The music got faster. Hannah moved her hands faster and faster over the keyboard. The dancers stopped and joined the rest of the skiers who were standing in front of the hole in the wall now looking in at Hannah.

"I never heard a kid play classical music like that!" said one of them. "She must be a child prodigy."

The music finished. The skiers applauded loudly. Hannah put her hands in her lap and looked down. She smiled.

All of a sudden the piano went "di da di *dum!*" and four keys went up and down by themselves.

"Oh, I forgot about that!" thought Hannah. The piano always played "di da di *dum!*" at the end, no matter what the roll was. Hannah quickly put her hands back up on the keyboard. But it was too late. The skiers had seen the keys go up and down without her hands on the keyboard.

"It's a player piano!" one of them yelled. They all burst out laughing. Hannah could feel her cheeks get hot. She wanted to jump up and run into her room and hide. But she looked up at the skiers and they looked so friendly through the hole in the wall, she stopped being so embarrassed.

"That was a good joke," said one of them to Hannah. "You really fooled us!"

Hannah ran into the kitchen instead.

"I'm finished," she said. "Can I push the sodas through the soda box?"

Her mother was running back and forth in the kitchen.

"I didn't expect so many customers today because of the snow," she said. "So I didn't make up any hamburgers in advance. It takes so long to make hamburgers for a gang. You watch the pot of water on the stove, Hannah, so the frankfurters don't burst open. Tell me when they look like they're getting fat. Oh—I just used the last hamburger roll. I'll have to cut the rest of the hamburgers in half and serve them on frankfurter rolls. Where is your father with those hamburger rolls? *That man is never around when I need him!*"

"The hot dogs are getting fat!" said Hannah.

"Here, you watch the onions a minute so they don't burn," said her mother. "Tell me when they start to get brown. Let's see, four want fried onions on their hamburgers, four want raw, two want pickle slices. I'll take out the hot dogs and put them on the rolls. Three with relish, one plain."

"The onions are getting brown," said Hannah.

"Okay," said her mother. "I'll take care of them. Here, you can bring out the frankfurters, then come back and I'll give you the hamburgers, then I'll bring out the coffee and French fries and you can push the sodas through the box and serve them."

"Yay!" said Hannah. She brought out the frankfurters and the skiers applauded again. She helped her mother serve the rest of the orders and she pushed the Coca-Colas through the soda box and put two straws in each bottle and served those too.

"I'll be back in a minute," said Hannah's mother, throwing a jacket around her shoulders. "They left their cars by the gas pumps so I could put in gas while they're eating. If anybody wants dessert, you can start waiting on them till I get back."

While Hannah's mother was outside pumping gas, the skiers ordered huckleberry, apple, and coconut custard pies with vanilla ice cream. Her mother had already sliced the pies in the morning, so Hannah took a pie knife, and very carefully she slid out the slices from the various pie plates and put them on plates. She took vanilla MelOrols out of the ice-cream box, unwrapped them, and put them on top of the slices of pie. Then she cleared the tables and served the desserts. When she had brought the last slice of pie over, the door opened and her mother rushed back in.

"I did all the desserts," said Hannah. "Oh— you're huffing and puffing. Your nose is red and you've got snow on your eyelashes."

"That's because all I have to do around here is

sit by the cash register and count the money," whispered Hannah's mother. Hannah giggled.

"Everything was just delicious," said one of the skiers. "We're nice and warm now, and not a bit hungry anymore. What do we owe you?"

Hannah's mother washed her hands and took a little pad. She wrote down all the hamburgers and frankfurters and coffees and sodas. Hannah told her how many pies and ice creams, and she added those in too. Then she added a dollar's worth of gas for each car.

The man who paid the bill said, "This is the nicest little restaurant on Route 9W. We'll be sure to stop here again."

He went over to Hannah and said, "And you're the best piano-playing waitress we ever had." He handed her a quarter.

"Wow!" said Hannah. "That's the biggest tip I ever saw! I can buy a big new box of crayons— with silver and gold!"

Just as everyone was saying good-bye, the door opened and Hannah's father came in. He was carrying two big brown paper bags.

"Here I am with the hamburger rolls!" he said. "Just in time."

"They're *leaving*," said Hannah's mother. "I had to use frankfurter rolls for half of the hamburgers."

"Good-bye!" The skiers waved. "See you again."

"I never expected so many customers in weather like this," said Hannah's father, setting the bigger bag down on the floor just below the hole in the wall, "or I would have brought the rolls back faster. You know how it is, you go into town, you see people. You start to talk." He put the other bag in the kitchen.

"The rolls weren't the biggest problem," said Hannah's mother. "It was making up all those hamburgers while I was trying to do a lot of other things—that's what took me so long. You should invent a mechanical person to make hamburgers, a whole bunch at a time, and that would save a lot of time and work."

"Not a bad idea," said Hannah's father. "But one patent at a time. I have to go back out to the car a minute to get something."

"Your father and his surprises!" said Hannah's mother. She began to clear the pie plates from the table. Hannah helped.

There was a knock on the restaurant door and Hannah went over and opened it. Her father was carrying something very large in his arms. "Thanks," he said to Hannah. "I had to hold on with both arms, so I couldn't open the door myself." He set down a great big glass tank on the floor next to the brown paper bag just below the hole in the wall.

"What's that?" asked Hannah and her mother both at the same time.

"You'll see," said Hannah's father. He went back out to the car and came back with a bunch of long metal pieces. He took off his coat and put the metal pieces together to make a frame with legs. Then he put the glass tank on top of the frame right in front of the hole in the wall.

"That's exactly the same size as the hole!" said Hannah. "Just a little extra space on the sides."

"Of course," said her father. "I planned it that way."

"Is that a fish tank?" asked Hannah's mother. "A great big fish tank?"

"It's an *aquarium*," said Hannah's father proudly.

"Oh, can I help pick out the fish?" asked Hannah.

"I bought a few goldfish already," said her father. "Just to get it started. You can help me put them in, along with the other stuff I got. Next week I'll take you to a special place in Jersey where we'll get some tropical fish."

"Fancy fish," said Hannah's mother. "That's all we need!"

"Sure," said Hannah's father. "It makes the place more cheerful." He took several little white containers out of the big brown paper bag. He gave Hannah a stool to stand on in front of the aquarium. They filled the bottom of the aquarium with colored pebbles from one container. From another, they got grassy green things and stuck them in between the pebbles. Hannah's father dropped in a few tiny snails. He gave Hannah a little castle to put in the middle.

"Oh—it looks like in a fairy tale," said Hannah.

Her father filled the aquarium with water. It took such a long time, Hannah's mother washed and dried all the dishes from the customers before the aquarium was full.

"Now," said Hannah's father. "The first four fish." Hannah's mother came over to watch. He gave Hannah a tiny fishnet with a long handle and he opened the last container. He let Hannah fish out the goldfish and put them into the filled aquarium. Hannah was very careful. She held her breath till the last fish was in. "Look how fast they swim," she said. She watched them dart back and

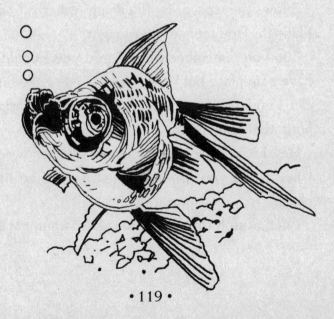

forth in the water. "Two oranges and two blacks," she said. "And all of them have gold underneath. It shines through."

"That's why they're called goldfish," said her father.

"Look at their pop eyes," said Hannah.

"Now comes the beauty of it," said Hannah's father. "Come into the living room." Hannah and her mother followed him into the living room.

"Oh, look how nice it looks right next to the picture of the waterfall," said Hannah.

"It's supposed to," said her father. He clipped two lights onto either side of the aquarium.

"Now the space is filled up exactly," said Hannah. "You measured just right."

"Do you remember when I told you I couldn't have a fireplace but I was working out something else I could sit back and stare at at night?" asked her father.

"Yes, I remember," said Hannah. "On Halloween, when I told you about the house with the fireplace."

"Well, watch this," said Hannah's father. He sat

down in his favorite chair right next to the hole in the wall that now had the aquarium right in front of it.

"Make believe it's nighttime," he said to Hannah. "It's dark. We turn out all the lights. Then I turn on these." He pushed a little switch on each light on the sides of the aquarium. The fish swam around and around. "One went into the castle," said Hannah. "It's hiding!"

"It's a *two-way aquarium*," said Hannah's father. "The customers can look in and see it from the restaurant. At night we can just sit and stare at it from the living room. Just picture it."

"Who wants to sit in the dark at night?" asked Hannah's mother. "At night I like to sit and read a book."

"But before reading," said Hannah's father. "Or after. It'll be *relaxing*. Like looking into a fireplace. You can watch things *move*."

Hannah closed her eyes. She pictured the room all dark with no lights on at all except the two clipped to the sides of the aquarium. In her picture everything was shining. The grassy things shone green. The fish shone orange and black and gold. They played hide-and-seek in the castle. "They're really princes and princesses," Hannah said to herself, "but a spell was put on them. From a *frog* hiding under the waterfall in the picture from Macy's."

"I never saw something like it," said Hannah's father.

Hannah opened her eyes.

"Neither did I," she said.

Hannah's Mother's Story

Hannah went over to the French doors in the living room and watched the falling snow.

"It looks so beautiful out there," she said to her mother. "The trees across 9W and the trees down below on the other side of the railroad tracks. Even the ugly sumac tree in your garden doesn't look as bad with snow on the branches." Her mother came over and looked out too.

"Your garden is all covered with snow," said Hannah. "I'm glad. Now you won't work out there and get any more poison sumac on your hands."

"But the garden is working by itself *under* the snow," said her mother.

"What do you mean?" asked Hannah.

"It's getting ready to grow," said her mother.

"In the wintertime?" asked Hannah. "Under the snow?"

"Under the snow and under the ground," said her mother, "roots are growing and getting ready to push up in the spring. Remember those things you called onions? Well, you may see something growing before the snow is even gone this year."

Hannah looked at her mother a minute.

"Why do you want a garden there anyway?" she asked. "That's an awful place on the side of a hill. It's crooked; it's hard to stand up. You work so hard on it besides all the work in the restaurant. And you got bad poison sumac on your hands from the sumac tree. You could get it again."

"Maybe I will get poison sumac on my hands again, but I'll take the precautions the doctor told me about. I'll wash with the brown soap after gardening to try to prevent it. If I get it anyway, I'll put calamine lotion on to stop the itch and keep it from spreading. And if that doesn't work, I'll put long rubber gloves on when I garden, but only if I have to. Because I like the feel of the dirt under my fingers. But not make a garden at all? No, I couldn't do that. I've waited so long, I have to garden. Come here, let's sit down. I'll tell you a story, if you feel like listening, and you'll know why."

"Okay, I'm sitting. Tell me! You *know* I love stories. *If* I feel like listening—what a funny thing to say!"

Hannah's mother began her story.

"A long time ago," she said, "when I was about twice as old as you are now, I was getting ready for my high school graduation. I was terribly sad."

"Why were you sad before your high school graduation?" asked Hannah. "I would think you would be glad."

"I was sad because I loved school very much and I didn't want to stop going. Every June I used to be sad when school was over, even when I was your age. The other kids used to jump in the air and yell 'hooray!' on the last day of school, but I used to go home and sit on the stoop of our building and cry."

"Why did you cry?"

"I cried because I didn't want school to end. When I was your age, I spent the rest of the summer on that stoop—when I wasn't inside making passementerie—trying to organize the rest of the kids on the block to play school. They were the pupils and I was the teacher."

"Oh—just like Grandma and me! I like to be the teacher too! But passementerie—what a nice word!—what is it?"

"Braided trimming for ladies' suits. Grandma used to do piecework to earn money at home."

"What's piecework? Why did she do it?"

"Grandpa worked hard, but his salary wasn't enough to feed Grandma, my three brothers, and me. So Grandma thought up an idea to earn extra money at home. She went into a little factory where they made passementerie and she talked the owner into letting her try to make the braided trimming at home and paying her for it by the piece. *That's* piecework. The owner didn't think she could do it, but he gave her a try. He gave her big spools of silk thread, all different colors."

"How did she do it?"

"She set up two big tables with spindles in our kitchen, one on one side of the room, and one on the other. The threads went from the spindles on one table all the way across to the spindles on the other. In the middle there was a spinning wheel that we pumped with our feet, just like you pump our player piano. When you pumped the spinning wheel, all the threads attached to the spindles got braided into beautiful shiny passementerie for ladies' suits. Grandma got my friend Rosie and me to help so we could get a lot done. She really surprised that factory owner. So not only Grandma earned extra money, but Rosie and I did too. Rosie was so good at it that when we grew up, she made a real passementerie shop of her own and it was a big success. But I wanted to be a teacher, so whenever I didn't have to help out with the passementerie in our kitchen, I ran down to the front stoop and called all the kids in our neighborhood to play school."

"Okay. Enough passementerie. Now finish the story about the last day when you were in high school."

"On the last day of school, I cried harder than ever. I wanted to be a teacher more than anything, but I knew I couldn't afford to go to college. I hadn't even been able to take the time to go to a regular high school. There was a school in New York City called Hebrew Technical School for Girls. It was a special school for smart girls from poor families. You had to have an A average to get in."

"Why?"

"Because you had to do four years of high-school work in three years."

"Did you?"

"Yes. That way I graduated a year sooner and went out to earn more money to help the family. Everybody had to help out. I became a bookkeeper."

"But you just said you wanted to be a teacher."

"I did. But I also said there was no way I could go to college to become a teacher. I had to earn money to help contribute to the family right then. Teacher was my first choice. I had to take my second. But I liked being a bookkeeper lots better than sitting in the kitchen making passementerie. Grandma used to say, 'We're poor, but my mother and father were poorer.' And then she said, 'I have it a little better than my mother did and you have it a little better than I do. And when you have a daughter she'll have it a little better than you.'"

"'When you have a daughter . . .' That's me!"

"That's right."

"Keep telling the story."

"Another thing I always wanted besides to be a teacher was to have a little garden."

"Why didn't you?"

"Where would we put it? We lived in a cold-water flat in a walk-up in New York City. There wasn't any ground."

"What's a cold-water flat?"

"An apartment with no hot water. We had to heat water in big pots on the kitchen stove."

"So finish telling the story on the last day of school."

"On the last day of school, a rich man came to our school to speak at our graduation. He was a famous philanthropist."

"What's a philanthropist?"

"A rich man who shares and gives things away to others who aren't rich."

"Oh, that's nice. What did he give?"

"First let me tell you what he said. He made a speech. He told us all he was proud of us. He said we were good students and hard workers. He told us all to go out into the world and keep up the good work. And then he said he had a surprise for us. Something to take home."

"What was it?"

"Wait a minute, I'll tell you. We all got our diplomas. Just before the principal read our names and handed us our diplomas, two big boys came out carrying big flat boxes. Inside the boxes were the surprises. As each graduate was called up to the stage to get a diploma from the principal, the rich man handed us our surprises."

"What were the surprises? I can't wait anymore."

"The big flat boxes were filled with tiny trees. Each tree had a ball of dirt that the roots were in, and a piece of burlap was tied around the roots so the dirt wouldn't fall off."

"Oh, a little tree—what a nice graduation present!"

"I cried and cried."

"Why did you cry? You just said you always wanted to have a little garden."

"I did. That's why I cried. I didn't have anyplace to put it. The rich man meant well, but he didn't realize how poor we all were. He lived in the country on a big estate with acres and acres of land. He didn't know there were some people so poor they didn't even have a few inches of ground to plant a tree in."

"What happened?"

"Most of the other kids thought it was funny. A lot of them were laughing after the rich man left. Nobody knew what to do with the trees. Some of the kids said, 'Who wants a dinky little tree?' But I cried because I *did*. In addition to crying because school was over for good and now I knew I could never really become a teacher."

"So what did you do?"

"I got lucky. I knew a boy named Joe whose father was the super of a building not too far away from ours. Joe's family lived in the basement apartment. There was a little bit of ground in a semicircle in front of one of the windows in their basement apartment. Joe came over to me and said, 'Don't cry, Mollie, I'll take your tree over to my house and plant it next to mine in that little piece of ground. Come over tomorrow and you'll see it.'"

"Did he? Did you?"

"The next day I had to go right out and look for a job. I looked all day and found one too. I was good in arithmetic, so I got a job as a bookkeeper. I knew my mother would be *proud* I could be a bookkeeper. She was already so proud because I had graduated from high school. I was hurrying home to tell her the news. And then I saw Joe coming toward me. He took my hand and said, 'I planted the tree, Mollie, and I named it after you.

So come and see the Mollie tree.'"

"Did you?"

"What a question! Of course I did. I watered that little tree every day all that summer before I started out for work. But now you see why I don't think my garden is awful, even on the side of a hill, even with that sumac tree in the middle. I was terribly disappointed when Daddy couldn't get the tree out because of the long roots. Sure, worrying about getting poison sumac takes some of my pleasure away. But I won't let it take all my pleasure away—because gardening is my pleasure. And that's why I have to do it. If I could have my dreams come true, the sumac tree would be out and instead, in the middle, I'd have a birdbath. Birds would be flying in and out, drinking and splashing and singing. I had a lot of dreams. But so does everybody. And the way I look at it is something is better than nothing. We own a piece of land, even though most of it is sloping down a hill. I've finally got a garden. And when I garden, I feel good, so instead of birds singing, *I'll* sing."

Hannah was quiet a long time.

"What are you thinking, Hannah?" asked her mother.

"I was thinking," said Hannah. "I wish I could see that Mollie tree."

"You can't do that," said her mother, "but wait until spring comes. Because then you'll see Mollie's garden. And now I'm going to start supper."

Hannah sat and looked out at the snow and was quiet some more. After a long time, she got up and went back to her room and rolled up the top of her rolltop desk. She sat down and took her pepper-and-salt book out of the drawer. She turned to page five, "Things I Might Be When I

Grow Up." She crossed out "I might be a waitress." She crossed out "I might be a movie star." She crossed out "I might be an artist." And she wrote, "When I grow up, I am going to be a teacher."

Hannah Is a Palindrome

There were two things in school Hannah had never been picked to be. The first was monitor when the teacher had to leave the room. The second was the person who clapped erasers together to clean the chalk dust out. "I wonder if Miss Pepper knows about that," thought Hannah.

So one morning she wrote a note in school, and it said:

Dear Miss Pepper,

Did you know that I was never monitor and also I never clapped erasers?

I wish I could do one or two of those things.

Because I am going to be a teacher.
Best of all, I'd like to be monitor.
                              Love,
                              Hannah
P.S. But I also like to clap erasers.

Then she went up to the pencil sharpener
and sharpened her pencil. On the way back to
her seat, she dropped the note on Miss Pepper's
desk.

Miss Pepper cleared her throat. She opened the
drawer at the top of her desk and took out a little
box. Hannah looked to see if it said "Cherry"
or "Licorice." All day long Miss Pepper sucked
on cherry or licorice cough drops. "I have a dry
throat," she always said. Hannah loved cherry *and*
licorice cough drops. She could never decide
which she liked better. When somebody was
monitor, if they kept the room quiet, Miss Pepper
would say, "Well done," when she got back. And
then she would say, "Would you like a cherry or
a licorice cough drop?" All the kids liked cough

drops. But no one except Miss Pepper or a good monitor could eat them in school without a note from a doctor.

Hannah dreamed of being monitor and being offered cherry or licorice, but in her dream she could never decide which. Sometimes Hannah still had trouble making up her mind. But she didn't want Miss Pepper to know that, because Miss Pepper had a rule, "Don't be indecisive." Hannah had looked up "indecisive" in the dictionary, and she decided that rule meant "Make up your mind."

The box said "Cherry," and Hannah licked her lips as Miss Pepper popped the cherry cough drop into her mouth.

Hannah said "mmm" to herself, but she didn't say it out loud. Miss Pepper had a lot of rules of good behavior in the classroom, and "Don't say 'mmm'" was one of them. In school, Hannah always tried to control herself and follow all Miss Pepper's rules of good behavior. At home, she acted natural.

Miss Pepper stood up.

"It is time for our new word of the day," she said. "It's a big one." Miss Pepper loved big words.

Otto Zimmer groaned.

Miss Pepper sucked on her cough drop and looked at Otto.

"Otto," she said, "you know the rules of good behavior in this class. And 'No groaning' is one of them."

Miss Pepper gave a new word every day. She had a special place on the blackboard to write it. She always wrote the new word in the special place and then she asked someone to look it up in the dictionary. Then that person had to tell the definition. Then everybody wrote it five times. And then they took it home for homework and wrote it five more times and made up a sentence with the new word in it.

All the children liked to be picked to be monitor or clap erasers. But nobody liked to be picked to look up words in the dictionary. Looking up words in the dictionary was hard. Miss Pepper's dictionary was fat and it was on a special dictionary stand in the corner. It was hard to make it stay open to the page you wanted. There was so much little print on each page, and it was easy to lose your place while you were looking back at the special place on the blackboard to see the word. If you lost your place, the pages flopped over and you had to start all over again. Once that had happened to Aggie Branagan three times in a row, and Aggie had burst into tears. Hannah had never been picked to be monitor or clap erasers. But Miss Pepper often called on her to look up new words. Hannah hated it, like playing scales on the piano.

"Today's word is a really hard one," said Miss Pepper. "Three syllables!" Hannah started to slump down in her seat so Miss Pepper wouldn't see her and call on her. But then she remembered the rule "Watch your posture; don't be a slumper," so she sat up tall.

Miss Pepper went to the blackboard. She picked up a piece of chalk. Under the place where it said "Word of the Day," she wrote *palindrome*.

"Who would like to look this word up in the dictionary?" asked Miss Pepper.

Everybody looked at the floor except some kids who looked at the ceiling. Aggie made believe she had dropped something and hid her head under her desk.

Miss Pepper looked around the room. "I'll give you a hint," she said. She looked at Hannah.

"Oh, no!" said Hannah to herself. "Not again!"

Under the word, Miss Pepper wrote, "Hannah is a palindrome."

Hannah was very surprised. She had never seen herself in a sentence before.

"What's a palindrome?" she wondered.

Miss Pepper raised her chalk to write again.

Just then the buzzer rang. That meant Miss Pepper had to leave the room.

"Who would like to be the monitor while I am gone?" she asked.

All the children raised their hands.

Hannah waved her hand round and round in the air. She wiggled a lot in her seat even though "Don't wiggle" was one of the rules of good behavior. But she wanted to be monitor so much. She also wanted to win a cherry or a licorice cough drop even though she couldn't decide which.

"Hannah," said Miss Pepper, "you have always been a conscientious student who follows the rules except for sometimes when you get the giggles. Being monitor is serious business. It means being the teacher when the teacher is away. If you're sure you wouldn't get the giggles, there is no reason why you shouldn't get a chance to be monitor." She looked at Hannah's note and added, "Also, it would be good practice for you."

Hannah almost flew into Miss Pepper's big chair in front of Miss Pepper's big desk.

"Now I know everyone will be quiet and do his or her word work till I get back," said Miss Pepper. "But if anyone breaks a rule of good behavior, Hannah, just write his or her name down on the blackboard."

Miss Pepper always said that.

The monitor always wrote names down on the blackboard. Besides wanting to feel like a teacher and get a cough drop, that was one of the reasons

Hannah wanted to be monitor so much. Before her grandmother had moved back to New York City, she had bought Hannah a blackboard. Hannah used to write her grandmother's name down when her grandmother talked. But that was just one name. And now she didn't even get to do that. So now Hannah wanted to be a real monitor in real school and write down a lot of real names. "I'll have fun," she thought.

"Remember all the rules of good behavior while I am gone," said Miss Pepper to the class. "Control yourselves. Do your word work. And act like little ladies and gentlemen. Hannah is your monitor."

Then she left the room.

As soon as the door closed, Otto made a rude noise. Otto always made rude noises when Miss Pepper left the room.

"Stop that, Otto," said Hannah. "You know the rules of good behavior in this classroom."

"Hannah is a palindrome!" said Otto.

"Oh, I am not," Hannah wanted to say. But it was written right on the blackboard.

Hannah wondered what a palindrome was. She

didn't want Otto to know she didn't know.

"No talking out, Otto!" said Hannah. "That's one of the rules and you know it. Who will look up today's word in the dictionary?"

"Raspberries!" said Otto.

"Otto!" said Hannah. "I'm warning you. I *mean* it, Otto."

Otto just made more raspberry noises.

"I'm serious, Otto," said Hannah. "I'll give you one more chance."

"Hannah is a palindrome!" said Otto.

"That's enough fooling around, Otto," said Hannah. "I gave you two chances already."

She picked up a piece of chalk and wrote

OTTO ZIMMER

on the blackboard. She wrote with her best penmanship because "Don't write with poor penmanship" was another one of Miss Pepper's rules. While Hannah was writing, the chalk squeaked.

"Eek!" said Otto, imitating the chalk.

"You want me to write your name down twice?" asked Hannah.

"Hannah is a palindrome!" said Otto.

"Otto! *No talking!*" said Hannah. "That's the most important rule!"

All Miss Pepper's rules were important, like "No getting the giggles, because you could pass it on to your neighbor," and "Never waste paper on a paper airplane, and if you do don't sail it." But some rules were more important than others.

"No talking" was the most important rule of all.

All of a sudden other kids were talking too.

"No talking!" said Hannah to the class. "I *mean* it. Now who is going to look up that word?"

But the kids who were talking kept right on talking.

"I'll give you one more chance," said Hannah.

But they kept right on talking.

"Hannah is a palindrome!" said Willie Hoffman.

Frankie Canelli and Eddie Bugbee said it right after him.

So Hannah wrote,

WILLIE HOFFMAN

FRANKIE CANELLI

under "Otto Zimmer."

Then Alfred Hennessy made a little paper airplane and sailed it across the room at Philip Higgle.

"No paper airplanes, Alfred," said Hannah. "Now who is going to look up that word?"

Philip Higgle sailed the little paper airplane back at Alfred Hennessy.

"Listen, Alfred and Philip," said Hannah, "I *mean* it. Stop sailing little airplanes."

So they made and sailed medium-sized ones instead.

Hannah wrote,

ALFRED HENNESSY
PHILIP HIGGLE

underneath "Otto Zimmer," "Willie Hoffman," "Frankie Canelli," and "Eddie Bugbee."

She tried to have good penmanship and have straight margins, because "Don't forget your margins" was in the rules too. While she was writing, an airplane landed on her shoulder. Hannah whirled around.

"Who made that airplane?" she asked.

Nobody answered.

Becky Jackson started to giggle. Aggie Branagan sat across from Becky and Aggie caught the giggles. Hannah usually giggled whenever Aggie did, but today Hannah didn't giggle. She just said, "Aggie!" and stared at her. "You're my *friend*," she tried to say with her eyes.

Aggie's face got very red. She said, "I'm sorry, but I can't help it, Hannah. You looked so funny with that airplane on your shoulder!" She put her hands over her mouth, but she didn't stop giggling. Becky giggled with her.

Hannah sighed. She knew she couldn't play favorites. So she wrote,

BECKY JACKSON
AGGIE BRANAGAN

Then she turned around and said, "Who is going to look up that word?"

Nobody answered.

They all started to talk, giggle, and sail airplanes instead.

It looked like a roomful of big white birds swooping and dipping all around Hannah's head.

One big airplane even sailed out the window.

Hannah clapped her hands together loudly, as Miss Pepper did when the room got too noisy. She even said, "This is disgraceful behavior!" the way Miss Pepper did, but no one heard her. They were too busy talking, giggling, and making and sailing paper airplanes. Hannah didn't feel one bit like giggling. She felt like putting her hat on her head, walking out of the room, and going home. But there was another rule, "Don't give up the ship." It meant "Keep trying."

So Hannah didn't give up the ship. She wanted Miss Pepper to say, "Well done," when she came back into the room, like she did to the other good monitors.

"Hannah is a palindrome!" yelled Otto.

Then everybody in the room said it with him—except Aggie. Aggie wasn't giggling anymore. But her face was still red.

Hannah wrote,

SUSAN SLOTNICK

MARTHA CARLSON

MARTIN MARKOWITZ

JOE ROBERTS

ALLEN GREEN

ROBERTA BLEIGLE

JOANN HIGGINS

ELMER JONES

JENNY RICHARDS

TESSIE SIMON

MELBA PRINGLE

Hannah's right arm was getting tired. Her penmanship was getting harder to read. Her margins weren't so straight anymore. "I don't like being monitor so much," she thought. She wished Miss Pepper would hurry up and come back and say, "This is disgraceful behavior!" to the rest of the class and "Well done, Hannah." Besides, there wasn't any more room on the blackboard to write more names. Also, there weren't any names left to write. Hannah had written the name of every kid in the class. But it was no fun.

"They'll really get it when Miss Pepper comes back," she thought. "Wait—maybe *I'll* get it. Maybe Miss Pepper will say, 'Why didn't you keep them quiet?' Maybe I won't get a cherry *or* a licorice cough drop."

"Who is going to look up that word?" said Hannah one more time. But she knew no one would answer. They were too busy yelling, "Hannah is a palindrome." Except Aggie. Aggie was sitting up tall now with her hands folded on her desk. She looked like she was going to cry. Hannah was sorry she had written Aggie's name on the blackboard and wished there was some way she could take it off without playing favorites.

An eraser sailed through the air.

"No throwing erasers!" said Hannah. "That's a rule!"

The biggest airplane of all sailed by. It said HANNAH IS A PALINDROME in great big capital letters that Hannah could read as it sailed by.

Everybody laughed except Hannah and Aggie. Hannah felt like crying, but she had one rule of her own: "Never cry in front of other kids."

"This is terrible," she said to herself. "How will I ever be a teacher? No one is even listening to me. I can't decide what to do."

All the kids except Aggie were up out of their seats sailing airplanes and throwing erasers. Aggie had her head hidden underneath her desk again.

Hannah walked over to the dictionary. No one even noticed her.

She looked up "palindrome." She read for a long time. More erasers and airplanes sailed by. Hannah ignored them.

After she had finished looking in the dictionary, she looked at Otto. She closed the dictionary and picked it up. It was very heavy.

Hannah carried it to Miss Pepper's desk.

"*Quiet!*" she said. "I looked up the word myself. I'm *telling* you something!"

THUMP! An eraser bounced off Hannah's head. Hannah forgot about the rule "Control yourself."

She slammed the big heavy dictionary down on Miss Pepper's desk. She slammed it down so hard she thought the desk would break in half. It made such a loud bang, even Hannah jumped. Aggie screamed. Otto's lower jaw flopped open.

And the room got quiet. The erasers stopped. The airplanes stopped. The kids sat down and stared at Hannah.

She picked up all the airplanes. She picked up all the erasers. She erased all the names so she would have room to write.

She picked up a new piece of chalk. Underneath where Miss Pepper had written the new word and the sentence, Hannah wrote, "Otto is a palindrome."

She wrote slowly and carefully. The chalk didn't squeak.

Otto's mouth fell open even wider.

Hannah turned around and faced the class.

"A palindrome," she said, "is a word that is

spelled the same backward as forward. Now write it five times and for homework use it in a sentence."

The room was very quiet.

The door opened and Miss Pepper walked in.

Miss Pepper looked all around.

"Why, what a lovely class," she said. "How nice it makes me feel to think you were so well behaved and quiet while I was gone. Not one name on the blackboard. And 'Otto is a palindrome'! Why, I was just about to write that on the blackboard myself when the buzzer rang. How clever of you to figure that out by yourself, Hannah. What a good teacher you are. Well done, Hannah. Would you like a licorice or a cherry cough drop?"

Hannah couldn't answer. All of a sudden she felt very tired. She went back to her seat and sat down. She put her head down on top of her desk. Inside the circle of her arms, she did some thinking. "What should I tell her?" she wondered. She was ashamed to accept a cough drop. Also, she still hadn't decided which flavor.

So she took out a piece of paper and wrote
Miss Pepper another note.
She wrote:

Dear Miss Pepper,

It wasn't really quiet while you were gone.

People talked and yelled and threw erasers and sailed airplanes.

I clapped my hands and stamped my feet and wrote all the names on the blackboard. There wasn't any more room to write so I had to erase.

Nobody would look up palindrome in the dictionary. So I looked up palindrome in the dictionary. That's how I figured out about Otto.

I didn't giggle. But I slammed the dictionary down on your desk.

It made a big bang.

Everybody jumped. I jumped too. And

that's how it finally got quiet.

It got quiet just before you came in the door.

I was a terrible monitor. I'll never be able to be a teacher.

Love,
Hannah

P.S. Do I still get the cough drop?

Hannah went up to the pencil sharpener again and sharpened her pencil till there was nothing left but a point on one end and an eraser on the other. She dropped the note on Miss Pepper's desk on her way back to her seat.

Miss Pepper read the note.

When she finished, she said, "Well, of all things! Hannah, this sounds just like a description of what happened to me on the very first day of the very first year I was a teacher! I know exactly how that feels. I slammed a book down like that myself! That's when I started to make Miss Pepper's Rules and Regulations of Good Behavior.

Now if there's one thing I like it's an honest person! You used your ingenuity—and that will be the new word for tomorrow. All right, Otto, stop that groaning. Would you like to clap the erasers together now, Hannah? And would you like a cherry or a licorice cough drop?"

Hannah stared at Miss Pepper. She had never heard her teacher say things like that before. She couldn't believe it—Miss Pepper talked like a real person!

After a while, Hannah got up. She took the erasers over to the window. She opened a window and clapped erasers together two at a time. Clouds of chalk dust went up in the air. Hannah coughed. She looked up and watched the chalk clouds float up toward the real clouds. The sky was bright, blue, and beautiful.

When all the chalk dust was gone, Hannah closed the windows. She put the erasers back. She went over to Miss Pepper's desk.

She looked at the little box that said "Licorice" and she looked at the little box that said "Cherry."

"I made a decision," said Hannah. "I'll have one of each, please."

Back at her desk, Hannah wrote one last note:

Dear Aggie,

Come to The Grand View Restaurant after we go home. We'll have an ice-cream cone and play school. And I'll give you one lick of each cough drop.

Love from your friend,
Hannah

P.S. I'll be the teacher, of course.

A Picnic on the Porch

Hannah sat outside at a round orange table with a hole in the middle of it. She ran her finger around the edge of the hole. In the center of the hole was a wooden umbrella pole. She touched the pole. She looked up. The big umbrella was wide open. It had orange and green stripes. Hannah stared up at the white fringe hanging down all around the edges of the umbrella.

"This is the fanciest table I ever sat at," she thought.

She looked down at the lined paper, the piece of drawing paper, and the box of crayons she had brought out with her, and she began to write.

Dear Grandma,

So much has happened since I wrote to you last, I don't know what to tell you first.

Spring is finally here. Hooray!

I can play five pieces on the piano by myself, not rolls. This week I got a new one, "The Beautiful Blue Danube." At last!

My father made an invention that makes nine hamburgers at one time! He nailed strips of wood together, half going across and half going up and down. When he showed us, I said, "What's that? It looks like a big tic-tac-toe." He rolled out hamburger meat—with a rolling pin! He pressed the invention down on top of it. He said, "You pick it up." I did. There were three rows of hamburgers, three in each row. My father said, "There! Nine hamburgers at one blow! How do you like that?" My mother said, "But they're square. Hamburger rolls are round." My father said, "So we'll serve them on bread. Bread is square." I said, "But I like hamburgers on hamburger rolls." My father cooked one square hamburger. My mother put it on a roll. She said, "The four corners stick out." I picked it up and ate the corners off. I said, "All you have to do is take four extra bites. It's delicious." My father made a sign:

EAT A DELICIOUS HAMBURGER
AT
THE GRAND VIEW RESTAURANT
AND GET FOUR EXTRA BITES.

All the customers love it. They like it even better than the last sign,

A CLEAN LIFE IS A LONG LIFE.
KEEP THIS PLACE CLEAN AND
LIVE LONGER.

And even my mother says it's lots easier making nine hamburgers at one time. Even if they are square.

I saved the best surprise for last. Remember the French doors that didn't go anyplace that I told you about? Well, now they go someplace! And I am on that place writing to you right now. It's a little porch. My father built it. The paint on the floor and the railings just dried yesterday and he bought a table with an umbrella—and tassels! He wanted to buy two but my mother said we can't afford to spend so much. I'm sitting at the table right now. I'm the first one, before any customers.

When you sit here, you can see my mother's garden. It's growing! I was the first one to see a flower, too. One day in March I saw something purple poking through the snow. When I called my mother, she said, "Remember those things you thought were onions when I planted in the fall? Well, they were crocus bulbs. And that's a crocus!" And the next day I saw a yellow one. Now all sorts of things are growing and my mother's in the garden right now pulling out weeds. I hope she doesn't get poison sumac again. I went down in the cellar when my father was inventing the hamburger thing and I told him he should make an invention to get rid of the sumac tree. He said, "One patent at a time."

Well, good-bye, Grandma.

Love,

Your Teacher Hannah

P.S. Do multiplication tables 5 and 10. Now I'll make you some pictures.

Hannah opened her box of crayons with sixty-four colors and started to choose her colors. "I'll draw the two-way aquarium and all the new tropical fish," she thought. "I forgot to tell her about that."

She took out a crayon, put it down, got up, and went over to the railing.

"Can we have a picnic lunch on the porch?" she called to her mother. "To celebrate."

Her mother looked up. "What are we celebrating today?" she asked.

"Everything," said Hannah. "'The Beautiful Blue Danube' waltz and the hamburger maker and the porch and the table with the umbrella and your flowers. I'd like us to be the first ones to eat out here."

"It's all right with me, but it will have to be an early lunch, before noon when the cars start stopping for lunch, because after that, Saturday gets so busy we won't have time to eat together."

"That's all right. I'll just make a quick picture for Grandma to put in with my letter. Then I'll go downstairs and tell Daddy about the picnic."

"Your Daddy is working on a masterpiece, he says, so don't waste your time trying to go down—he won't let anyone in."

"He'll let *me* in," said Hannah to herself.

She drew the aquarium and used her gold crayon underneath the colors of the goldfish. She turned her picture over and drew a picture of her mother bending down in the garden on the side of the hill, wearing the funny hat that looked like an upside-down ice-cream cone. She drew the gardening gloves her mother was wearing to protect her hands from the sumac tree. She drew the sumac tree. "Ooh, that tree is ugly!" she said. She took a pencil and wrote underneath, "I'm not allowed in the garden because I might get poison sumac like my mother does. That tree is the enemy. But all up and down the hill, the beautiful flowers are growing. So my mother is the winner." Hannah drew flowers around the tree and colored them pink, yellow, and lavender.

"Now I'll draw the table with the umbrella on the porch," she thought. "I'll get another piece of paper from my rolltop desk."

She got up and went inside. When she passed the piano, she stopped and looked at her newest music sheet. "The Beautiful Blue Danube," she read out loud. "Simplified Version." She stopped and picked out a few notes.

Suddenly Hannah heard, "Psst!"

She looked around. She heard it again. This time it was a little louder and a little longer. She followed the sound. *"Pssst!"*

She walked all the way through the living room to the bathroom. The bathroom door was open. So was the trapdoor. Her father's head was sticking up.

"Was that you?" asked Hannah.

Her father motioned to Hannah to come over. He put his fingers to his lips.

Hannah tiptoed over.

"I don't want Mother to hear me," whispered Hannah's father. "Can you figure out a way to get her out of her garden? I'm working on my masterpiece and I have to go out in the garden to do something, but I don't want Mother to see. I need someone to keep her busy."

"I can keep her busy," said Hannah. "I asked her if we could have a picnic lunch on the porch, all together, and she said it's okay with her but it has to be early, before noon when the cars start stopping for lunch. I could ask her to come in and make the picnic lunch with me."

"Good," said Hannah's father. "Keep her *very* busy. And don't let her go back out till I call you, even if you hear noises. She can't go out on the porch either, or she'll see."

"See what?" asked Hannah.

"My masterpiece."

"I'd like to see the masterpiece," said Hannah. "Just once I'd like to see something before anybody else."

"It's a secret from Mother."

"I'll keep the secret. *I can keep a secret.* I'll show you. I won't say anything. Please—let me see!"

"All right, come down," said Hannah's father. "You'll see the masterpiece, but you still won't know the whole secret. I'll still have half a secret. I'm bursting already waiting to show it to somebody anyhow. When I'm done with this one, I'll be finished with all my surprises for this year."

"You always say that every time you work on something in the cellar."

"Well, summer is coming. Summer is the busy season in a restaurant on the highway. We'll get so busy Mother won't be able to just sit at the cash register anymore, so I'll have to stay upstairs and save all my new patents for next fall. Okay, you can come down for a minute—but only a minute. Then go up and keep Mother busy till I give the signal."

Hannah followed her father down the stairs. She saw a lot of things lying on and around his worktable. She saw a little silver box, a long post, a big bag, a wheelbarrow, and a hatchet. But then she saw something right in the middle of the worktable, and after she saw that, she couldn't look at anything else.

"Oh, a little wooden house!" said Hannah. "That's the cutest little wooden house I ever saw! Did you really make that yourself? It's so fancy!"

"Did I really make a porch?" asked Hannah's father. "And nine hamburgers at one blow? And a two-way aquarium that you can see from both sides? And a trapdoor to the cellar? So why not a little wooden house?"

"It's just like The Grand View Restaurant! It even has a little porch on the side!"

"I made the railings with lollipop sticks."

"Oh, can I have it?"

"Sorry, I have other customers for this little house," said Hannah's father mysteriously. "But you'll be able to keep seeing it. And that's all I'm going to tell you for now. Now you know *half* the secret. Just be sure you don't say a word to Mother. You always say you can keep a secret— now's your chance to prove it."

"Okay," said Hannah. "You'll see how I can keep a secret."

"Remember," said Hannah's father. "Get Mother inside and keep her busy till I give the signal."

"What's the signal?"

"I'll give a big loud whistle."

"Okay," said Hannah. "See you later." She went back up the steps and into the house through the trapdoor. She closed the trapdoor, and then she went through the living room and out onto the porch. She folded her picture and her grandmother's letter together and put her crayons back in the box.

"Time to start the picnic lunch now," she called to her mother.

"I'll be there in just a minute."

"Please come now. You said we have to eat early, before noon when the cars start stopping."

Hannah's mother picked up her hand rake and stepped from her garden to the outside stairs. She opened the gate at the top of the stairs and went around to the front door of the restaurant. "I was going to water the garden," she said, "but I'll do that later." She took off her gardening gloves and washed her hands with brown soap at the kitchen sink.

"I hope I didn't catch anything from that rotten tree," she said. She put her gardening things away and took a large brown-wrapped package out of the refrigerator.

"Fresh hamburger meat," she said.

"Can I use the new invention?" asked Hannah.

They heard loud noises from the cellar.

"That's your father working on his masterpiece," said Hannah's mother. "I don't know if you'll be able to get him to stop long enough to have a picnic lunch."

"He said he would," said Hannah. "I already asked him."

Hannah's mother rolled out the hamburger meat with her rolling pin. Then she handed the hamburger maker to Hannah. Hannah brought it down with a bang.

"There—nine at one blow!" she said.

"Some for us and some for customers," said her mother. She took six of the hamburgers and made a neat little pile with pieces of waxed paper in between. She put them back in the refrigerator. The other three she began to fry for the picnic lunch.

"Would you rather have French fries or baked beans?" she asked Hannah.

"Potato chips," said Hannah. "Because it's a picnic.

And pickles and *sodas*—okay? For a special occasion. To celebrate the new masterpiece and all the other nice things."

"Okay," said her mother. "Get me a Coca-Cola. Give your father, the masterpiecemaker, a grape, that's his favorite. And you take your choice."

Hannah went out to the front counter in the restaurant. She took a warm Coca-Cola, a warm grape, and a warm sarsaparilla from the neat piles underneath. She turned to the soda box and opened the metal flap on the right. She pushed each warm bottle through the tube that had that flavor. The flap on the left came up and out came cold Coca-Cola, grape, and sarsaparilla from the other side.

"Hooray!" said Hannah. "Ice-cold sodas!"

Suddenly Hannah heard loud noises from outside. She ran into the kitchen to make sure her mother was still busy with the hamburgers. But the stove was turned off and her mother wasn't there.

"Oh, look!" she heard her mother call. "The tree! *The tree is falling down!*" Hannah ran into the living room and looked out the French doors with her mother. They both ran out on the porch. Her father was standing on the hillside swinging an axe. Crash! The sumac tree came down. It rolled over and over down the hill and landed at the bottom, next to the railroad tracks.

"You chopped the tree down!" called Hannah's mother. "Hallelujah!"

"You weren't supposed to come out yet!" said Hannah's father. "Hannah was supposed to keep you inside."

"I tried!" said Hannah. "I didn't tell the secret about the masterpiece. But I was just getting our sodas for the picnic."

"It's all right," said her father. "You couldn't help it. I didn't bring out my masterpiece yet anyhow. But go back in now—I don't want you to see it till I'm ready. This way you'll get two surprises— even better!"

Hannah and her mother went back inside.

"Don't look!" said Hannah. "We promised."

"I can't believe that tree is down," said Hannah's mother. "I won't have to wear gloves anymore. Or wash with brown soap. I can put my hands right into the dirt, the way I like."

"And now could I plant green peppers?" asked Hannah.

"But the roots are still in the ground," her mother said. "Maybe we could still get poison sumac. I wonder. . . ."

They heard more noises. And still more.

"Don't go out and look," said Hannah. "I don't want Daddy to think I can't keep my promises. I promised to keep you busy inside."

They went back into the kitchen and continued preparing the picnic lunch. Hannah's mother finished cooking the three hamburgers. Then she cut the hamburger rolls in half and put the hamburgers inside. "Three square hamburgers," she said.

"With four extra bites apiece," said Hannah.

"Hannah," asked her mother, "what's the masterpiece?"

"You want me to tell a *secret*?" asked Hannah. "I promised to wait for the signal."

Hannah got the three cold sodas. Her mother opened them. Hannah got the ketchup bottle.

Her mother got the pickle jar.

Suddenly there was a loud whistle from outside.

"That's the signal!" said Hannah. "We can go look now."

They both ran through the living room and out the French doors to the porch.

Hannah's father was standing where the tree used to be. He had the proudest smile Hannah ever saw.

They looked where the tree had been. Something else was standing there besides Hannah's father. A long white pole—with the masterpiece on the top.

"A *birdhouse!*" said Hannah's mother. "In the garden!"

"*That's* what the little house was for!" Hannah said to her father. "The birds are the 'other customers.' How did you get it up so high on that pole?"

"I nailed it on," said Hannah's father. "Then I drilled a hole in the stump of the tree. I filled the hole with cement so the roots can't keep growing. I put the pole in the cement. I've been working on this patent for weeks. How do you like it?"

"I love it," said Hannah. "It's the fanciest bird-house I ever saw. It *is* a masterpiece. But what's that shiny silver thing inside the lollipop-stick porch? I didn't see that in there before."

"That's the beauty of it," said Hannah's father. "That's the best part of the whole masterpiece. Wait—you'll see." He carefully stepped around the flowers over onto the cement steps. At the top step, he attached a hose to an outside faucet and aimed it at the birdhouse.

"Watch this," he said. The water went up in the air in an arc, and when the sun hit the droplets of water, Hannah saw shimmering rainbow colors. "Just like in the picture from Macy's," she said to herself. When the spray came down, it landed right in the shiny silver-colored box.

"That's made of galvanized metal so it won't get rusty," said Hannah's father.

"A little silver bathtub for birds," said Hannah.

Her father turned off the faucet and took the hose off.

"I'll refill it every week," he said.

"A birdbath!" said Hannah's mother.

"I tried to plan a *regular* birdbath," said Hannah's father. "I know you wanted one. Hannah told me. But a regular-style birdbath wouldn't work out right on the side of a hill. It might flop over and roll down. But this wooden pole, cemented into the stump of the tree, will stand up straight. Look, the cement is almost hard already."

"This is a *better* birdbath," said Hannah. "It's a birdhouse and a porch and a little silver bathtub all in one!"

"Hungry, thirsty birds can stop here and eat, drink, and even sleep," said her father. "I'll plant a sunflower by the new fences I made near the zinnia seeds I planted. Birds love sunflower seeds."

"A birdhouse and a birdbath and a garden," said Hannah's mother quietly. "And no more sumac tree. I can't believe it." She looked at Hannah's father. "Thank you," she said.

"It's some masterpiece, if I do say so myself," said Hannah's father. "And you're welcome."

"*Now* can I plant green peppers?" asked Hannah.

"I don't see why not," said her mother. "But quick—come eat lunch first, before the hamburgers get cold. Before customers start to come."

"Yay!" said Hannah.

Hannah's father came into the house and washed his hands. Then they each carried something out to the porch and set the table. They sat down at the table underneath the umbrella.

"Eat," said Hannah's mother.

"We're all sitting together on the new porch," said Hannah. "We're having a celebration." She picked up her hamburger and opened her mouth, but before she could take even one bite, she heard a rumble. It got louder.

"The eleven twenty-seven train!" said Hannah's mother. "We forgot all about the train! Oh, my goodness—we'll get cinders all over the picnic!"

"Quick!" said Hannah's father. "Cover your hamburgers with your hands! Close your eyes! *Quick!*"

They covered their hamburgers with their hands and closed their eyes. The train roared by. The porch vibrated. The chairs with Hannah and her mother and father on them jiggled. The umbrella pole rattled. The table jumped. A potato chip flew up in the air and landed on Hannah's arm. She kept her eyes closed.

"Okay," said her father.

They opened their eyes. Their hands and arms were covered with little black specks. They shook their hands and blew the cinders off the table.

"We forgot all about the train!" said Hannah's mother. "Customers won't be able to eat out here!"

"Why not?" asked Hannah's father. "How often does the train pass by? There won't be another one till suppertime."

"But the cinders!"

"Most picnics have ants. So what's a few cinders?"

"You could get one in your eye."

"I'll make a sign for the porch: CLOSE YOUR EYES AND COVER YOUR SQUARE HAMBURGERS WHEN THE TRAIN PASSES BY. It'll be part of the fun. Enjoy the picnic!"

Hannah looked over at the side of the hill. The flowers were still vibrating. "Oh, look at your garden," she said to her mother. "Your flowers are *dancing!*"

Then Hannah and her mother and father all began to laugh at the same time. They laughed and laughed.

Hannah looked at the garden and the bird-house, and the little birdbath inside the lollipop-stick porch of the birdhouse, and the side of the hill that was turning all pink and yellow and lavender. Then she looked at her mother and father. She remembered once her grandmother told her you could take a picture inside your head and keep it there forever. Snap! Hannah took the picture.

"Oh, I like it here at The Grand View Restaurant," she said. "I really *like* it here."

And she ate the four corners off her hamburger.